My Mum and the
Hound from Hell

'OK. That does it. I can't take it any more.
Mum wants to add a dog to this overcrowded
collection of weirdos! The last thing we need
is a dog!'

Kate predicts trouble when her eccentric
Mum adopts a friendly but badly behaved pet.
Add to that the arrival of a gorgeous new boy at
school and the very odd behaviour of her best
friend, Chas, and Kate starts wondering if she's
going crazy…

Meg Harper has a varied life, writing, teaching
drama, home-educating her children and
helping to lead her church. In her spare time
she enjoys swimming, walking her dogs,
reading and visiting tea shops.

Other titles in this series: *My Mum and Other
Horror Stories* and *My Mum and the Gruesome
Twosome*.

For Emily and Miriam – with love

My Mum
and the
Hound
from Hell

Meg Harper

LION
Children's Books

Text copyright © 2003 Meg Harper
This edition copyright © 2003 Lion Publishing

The author asserts the moral right
to be identified as the author of this work

Published by
Lion Publishing plc
Mayfield House, 256 Banbury Road,
Oxford OX2 7DH, England
www.lion-publishing.co.uk
ISBN 0 7459 4799 9

First edition 2003
10 9 8 7 6 5 4 3 2 1

A catalogue record for this book is available
from the British Library

Typeset in 11/16 Garamond ITC Lt BT
Printed and bound in Great Britain
by Cox and Wyman Ltd, Reading

Contents

1

My Mum and the Hound from Hell

OK, that does it. Enough's enough. There's only so much a girl can take. I have finally had it. I have survived thirteen years living in this demented household but I can't take any more. It has come. The limit. The last straw. The final frontier. If I'm found one day foaming at the mouth as I try to leap off a tower block, then these files, painstakingly typed into this computer, will tell my story.

Meet my family:

1. Jo Lofthouse – apology for a mother. Variously known as Big Bum Mum (for obvious reasons), Big Tum Mum (when she was pregnant) and currently Big Dumb Mum or BDM for short (you'll soon see why!). Divides her time between being a part-time vicar and a full-time pain in the neck.

2. Phil Lofthouse – I used to think he was quite a cool dad. Has a very successful hairdressing business, a greying ponytail and an irritating habit of always being right (or thinking he is, anyway).

3. Ben Lofthouse – younger brother. Used to do nothing except read *Asterix* and play on the computer. Then had incurable attack of Humongous Hormones. Now does nothing except slaver over girlfriend Suzie and gel his hair. Owns psychopathic cat called Frisk.

4. and 5. Hayley and Rebekah – twin baby sisters. Rebekah quickly got nicknamed Comet (Halley's Comet – get it?) when she was smaller and did projectile puking (that's when it comes out so fast it splatters the walls). Actually, she hasn't changed much. Neither has Hayley.

6. Gran – very old, very frail but very feisty. Just lives in a slightly different world from the rest of us. It sounds very tempting.

7. Nic – our MALE French au pair. Yes, I know. You don't get many male au pairs – except in my family, of course. Says it all, really.

And now, to add to this overcrowded collection of weirdos (OK, so Gran's in a nursing home but that's only one less),

Mum proposes to add – wait for it – a dog! A DOG!

Don't get me wrong, I'm not a dog-hater. I'm not the sort of evil villain who throws puppies out of car windows on motorways. Basically, I'm a kind and long-suffering person – but (and it's a big BUT) – I have my limits. And the last thing we need in this house is a dog!

Mum doesn't think so.

'I'm on maternity leave, I've got Nic to help me, it'll be lovely for the twins, it's the ideal time really…'

She goes on and on. You'd think she'd been crying out for a pet-pooch since she was two years old! If she had, I'd be more sympathetic. But she hasn't. She does like dogs – in fact, she's the sort of sad person who sits glued to Crufts on the box once a year – but she's always said she hasn't the time or the energy to look after one properly – until now, that is.

The difference is that now there's a dog, 'free to a good home', living right next door! Well, he was next door until two weeks ago. And he's not some cute little puppy. He's a huge great lolloping black thing – like a Labrador crossed with something bigger and hairier. What's more, Ben's cat, Frisk, regularly reduces him to whimpers, so how's that going to work for a start? I should feel sorry for the poor pooch really, I know I should. It's a very sad story.

Mr Ponsonby our next-door neighbour, retired last year. To keep him company and to get him out and about, he got Rover. (Yes, Rover. If I've got to live with a dog, at least it could have a more original name!) Then, two weeks ago, Mr Ponsonby keeled over and died! He was only mowing the lawn and he had a massive heart attack. Which leaves Rover. Boneless. Kennel-less. Abandoned. None of Mr Ponsonby's relatives wants him so at the moment he's at the dogs' home – but not for much longer if BDM has her way.

'Mr Ponsonby was a lovely man,' she keeps saying, 'and he adored Rover. He'd be heartbroken if he knew what had happened to him.'

That's just typical of the stupid things BDM sometimes says. Does it really matter what Mr Ponsonby would think if he knew what had happened? Presumably he doesn't or heaven wouldn't be the blissful place it's cracked up to be. If you ask me, it's just a jolly good excuse for BDM to launch into a new project. She's like that – bell-ringing, abseiling, scuba-diving, belly dancing – you name it, she's done it.

Now I need to be mature and sensible about this. It's no good having a tantrum. I need to write a list of well-thought-out reasons why we shouldn't adopt Rover. I need to present the list to Mum and Dad in a calm and adult manner and suggest that they give it their due thought and consideration.

They weren't impressed. OK, so p'raps I did overdo it on the smelly reasons – you know, smelly dog breath, smelly dog food, smelly wet dog, smelly… I don't think I need to go on. But what about the expense? That's a perfectly good reason! And what about the fact that Ben and I are already on rotas for bathing babies, changing nappies, laying tables, clearing tables – you name it, there's a rota for it. The last thing we need is a dog-walking rota! *And* there's the fact that it's always a man and his DOG that finds bits of bodies in ditches when there's been a murder. Do they care? No. I even tried the how-do-you-justify-feeding-a-dog-when-children-are-starving? tactic. I thought that one was bullet-proof. I mean, Mum has a T-shirt that says 'The way you spend your money controls the world' (she has T-shirts saying everything from 'Make tea not war' to 'Fat Willy's Surf Shack' actually). But no. Somehow they managed to slime their way round that one too.

I'd tackle Dad on his own about it but he seems as keen on the idea as Mum. I can't quite work out why. When she wanted to keep a pig, he completely put his foot down. And let's face it, a pig snuffling round your garden eating leftovers is a whole lot more useful than a dog bounding round your house chewing everything in sight. Not great on the smell factor though. I wonder if there's something Dad knows that I don't?

I tried enlisting Ben's support – in one of those rare moments when he wasn't snogging Suzie or glued to his mirror. He was lying on his bed with his headphones on and – get this – a face pack! That's what happens to you if you hit puberty early. He might be hunkier than nearly all

11

the other Year 7 boys but he's absolutely paranoid about his spots. (I haven't got any. Ha-ha-di-ha.)

'Ben,' I said, 'about this dog idea…'

Ben skewed his eyeballs to look at me.

'I like dogs,' he grunted, barely moving his lips in case the face pack cracked.

'But Ben – Rover! He's a half-trained lunatic!'

'Nice dog. Very friendly.'

'*Too* friendly. If he isn't trying to knock me over, he's got his nose between my legs.'

'Take it as a compliment.'

'Ben, be serious! Do you want to be on a dog-walking rota?'

'Don't mind. Suzie could come. She loves dogs.'

I know when I'm beat. Suzie's dad's a vet. She loves anything that isn't human – which explains her devotion to Ben, I guess. If Ben sees dog-walking as another opportunity to snog Suzie then I might as well give up.

Life in this madhouse with a dog – no – with Rover, the Hound from Hell, I really don't think I can stand it. Boarding school would be preferable.

What did I write? What *did* I write? I can't believe it. It's like I tempted fate or something! Weren't things bad enough? Sometimes I feel like taking Mum on one side and re-arranging her brain – then p'raps she wouldn't keep on about how God loves us. 'All things work together for the good of those who love him' – meaning God! It's one of her favourite verses. Ha! OK, OK, so I've been through this before – this feeling that if there is a God, he gets a kick out of tormenting me – but really! Mum's going to have a jolly hard time convincing me there's a silver lining to this particular cloud.

Chas, my best friend in the whole world, has just rung. His parents are packing him off to boarding school! I can't believe it! First Rover – and now this! I'm going over there. They can't do this to him – to me! I've got to persuade them not to do it – now – before they buy the uniform or anything stupid like that! What on earth do they think they're doing?

It didn't take me very long to get there. For once, my bike lights were working and I cycled like a bat out of hell. (Question: why a *bat* out of hell? Wouldn't *anything* leaving hell want a quick get-away? Why not a cat? Or a DOG?)

Chas was on the lookout for me and dragged me towards the old outhouse he has for a den.

'But I want to talk to your mum and dad!' I protested.

'I know you do,' he said calmly, 'but you can't go barging in there yelling at them. You know what Mum's like.'

I certainly do. Ben and I call her Mrs Charming Peterson because she's the most fussy, gushy person we've ever had the misfortune to meet. And, despite being married to a farm-manager, she likes everything to be immaculate. I bet she even polishes her Hunter wellies! The only place Chas is allowed to make a mess is his den and Mrs Charming shudders every time it's mentioned. Really, I knew that bursting into her house, all hot and sweaty and windswept, would go down like pig-swill on her pristine beige carpet.

I followed Chas into his den, where he shoved aside a couple of cats and collapsed onto the old sofa he keeps there.

'Well?' I said, too wound up to sit down. 'What are we going to do?'

'Do? There's nothing *to* do. They're not going to change their minds. I've been lucky to escape this long.'

'Chas! Don't be so pathetic! You can't just take it lying down like that! You've got to fight!'

'You think I haven't? They sprang this on me on New Year's Day. Happy New Year, Chas – not! I've been fighting ever since.'

'But why didn't you tell me? I could've… I could've…'

'Could've come round and told them what you thought? Nice try, Kate. Thanks, but no thanks. You're one of the things they want to get me away from.'

'What? But I thought your mum liked me!'

'Oh, she does like you – as much as she likes anyone round here – but she thinks we're too close. She thinks I ought to have more chance to mix with "a different sort of girl" as she puts it.'

'What? The sort that's in the pony club and talks about tennis and croquet, you mean?'

'Got it in one.'

'Your mother is such a…' I stopped, not wanting to be too rude.

'Snob. Yes, I had noticed.' He looked away, biting his lip. I didn't know what to say. We'd been here before. I was forever moaning about BDM, always forgetting that Chas had an even worse time in a different way.

'I'm sorry, Chas,' I mumbled. 'I'm just so furious with her.'

'Me too – but there's nothing I can do about it – and neither can you. She's made up her mind.'

'But what does your dad think? Won't he miss your help round the farm?'

Chas shrugged. 'You know what he's like. As long as his pigs are happy, so's he. Anything for a quiet life. And *he* went to boarding school. Says it didn't do *him* any harm.'

I seethed quietly. *Didn't do him any harm!* Chas's father is probably the most boring person I know in the entire world. How Chas turned out so nice, I will never know. Frankly, I'm convinced he was adopted.

'Well, don't you have to take an exam to get in or something?' I said, clutching at straws. 'How can it suddenly all be sorted?'

'I took the exam, last year, remember? No, you probably don't, what with your mum's accident and the babies coming and everything.'

Now he came to mention it, I did vaguely remember but he was quite right – last year was a nightmare. Mum started it with a fractured skull and finished it with baby twins!

'Anyway, the school has a place for me and Mum says she's had enough of state schools so I'll have to go.'

'But it's not as if you're doing badly! You work really hard!'

'It's just an excuse. She says she's worried about teacher shortages and bad AS level results but really she just wants me to go to a posh school and meet posh kids.'

'And then *she* can go to posh garden parties and posh tennis tournaments and have sherry with the headmaster by the posh croquet lawn!' I raged.

Our eyes met. We both knew I had hit the nail on the head. It didn't help.

A couple of hours later, I cycled home slowly, my brain on overload. Mum and Dad were just going to have to forget Rover for the moment; they simply had to do something about Chas. Mrs Charming likes Mum – she was really helpful when Chas's grandad died – so we quite often get invited over for lunch. And I'll say this for Mum – she does have a way with people. Very useful in a vicar. She even has a way with me when she tries. So I wasn't going to give up hope. Not until Mum had given Mrs Charming a good going-over. That was the plan, anyway.

I put my bike away and opened the door.

'Mum!' I yelled and then – whumph! A shaggy black hearthrug hit me in the chest and started slavering all over my face.

Mum wasn't far behind. 'Down, Rover! Kate doesn't need her face washing! Down, I said!'

But Rover had no intention of getting down. Every time I grabbed his paws and plonked them firmly on the floor, he promptly jumped up again.

'Bad dog, Rover!' said Mum, hauling him off me. 'Get in your crate!'

Then she shoved him into this huge metal cage thing which had taken over our hall and was already festooned with drying baby clothes. She slammed the door shut and slotted the catches home. Rover gave us a reproachful look and then, miraculously, snuggled down on his blanket, his nose between his paws.

'He'll be all right for a bit in there,' said Mum breathlessly. 'He's over-excited – all these people, after the dogs' home.'

My brain felt as if firecrackers were going off inside it. One minute I'd been all set to sort out one crisis – and now my other crisis was gazing at me with huge sad eyes in my own hall!

'You… I… Chas…' I stammered. I had to do something about the Chas crisis quickly – but surely, surely they hadn't brought Rover home to stay without telling me first?

'Is *he* just here to see how he likes it?' I asked warily.

'Who? Rover? No, Kate. You know he's here to stay.'

'I know no such thing. I told you exactly what I think. You can't just go and get him without… without…'

'Without your permission?'

'No… I mean, yes… I mean… well, I should have been consulted. And what's that cage thing? You're not keeping him in there, are you?'

'Kate, you *have* been consulted. Your father and I have heard everything you've said and we still think it's a good idea to adopt Rover. And that cage thing is a puppy-crate. They're highly recommended these days – Mr Ponsonby bought it for Rover.'

'You might have *heard* me, but you haven't *listened*.'

'We *have* listened. We just don't happen to agree with you.'

'Well, you should have told me he was coming this evening.'

'We didn't *know* he was coming this evening. The dogs' home suddenly rang and asked if we'd made up our minds yet. They had a bit of a crisis with space.'

'You should've phoned me!'

'We *did* phone you. Didn't you get our message? I spoke to Chas's mum.'

'I never went into the house.'

'Kate! You never even said "hello" to Chas's mum? That was a bit rude!'

'Rude! You should hear what *she*'s gone and done. I never want to speak to her again! And I never want to speak to you or Dad again either. What's the point? Parents! You're all the same! You never listen!'

And with that, I stamped up the stairs to my room. That's where I am now. All I want to do is bawl my eyes out. Ha! I can hear a baby crying. Good. That'll teach them. Serves them jolly well right.

2

My Mum and the Sock-Snatcher

That first night with Rover was appalling. He really did seem out to prove that he was the Hound from Hell. Howl? I didn't know the meaning of the word before – and I thought the twins were bad enough.

It started when Mum took him out into the garden for a last wee. Suddenly, he must have realized where he was – next door to his old home. Either that or he noticed Frisk slinking into the house, her nose in the air. He just stood there on the patio and let rip!

'OK, so we've adopted a werewolf,' said Ben. 'Typical.'

'It isn't full moon,' snapped Mum, trying to haul Rover back into the house.

'I thought vicars didn't believe in werewolves,' I quipped.

'Ha ha, very funny. Could one of you two comedians give me a hand here, please?'

'After you, Ben,' I said. 'You wanted him.'

Twenty minutes and three cold sausages later, Rover was back in his crate – but he hadn't shut up. At any moment I expected the RSPCA to arrive and run us in for cruelty.

'We'll just have to leave him and go to bed,' said BDM. 'I'm sure he'll soon settle down and he doesn't seem to be disturbing the babies.'

Famous last words. At that precise moment, Hayley let out a wail fit to waken the dead – or Comet as it turned out, in this case.

Half an hour later, with Mum still busy trying to feed the babies off to sleep again, Dad, Nic, Ben and I were holding a council of war in the kitchen. We had let Rover out of his crate, fed him every scrap of dog-friendly food we could find (and some that wasn't), cuddled him, played with him and sworn at him and he was still howling.

'Right,' said Dad. 'Shut your eyes, everyone, and pray.'

We did. Rover carried on howling.

'What does it say in Jo's dog book?' said Nic.

Ever since she thought of rescuing Rover, Mum has been reading a book called *The Perfect Puppy*. I couldn't take it seriously. I mean – Rover? A puppy?

'The principles are the same,' she insists. 'And it's the book Mr Ponsonby was using. We ought to be consistent.'

'Good idea, Nic,' said Dad. 'Where is it?'

Ten minutes later we found the book. I flicked through it feverishly.

'According to this, he might be comforted by something that smells of his pack-leader. That used to be Mr Ponsonby. It's Mum now – so she says.'

'Well, it's worth a try,' said Dad. 'What could we use?'

We all gazed at the mountain of dirty laundry beside the washing machine. Dad grabbed the first item of Mum's which came to hand – a rather grubby-looking sock.

'Well, she won't miss this,' he said and offered it to Rover.

Maybe Rover was tired. Maybe he was hoarse. Maybe he realized that these stupid humans really weren't going to take him back to his real home and nice old Mr Ponsonby. I mean, what would you conclude if you howled for a couple of hours and then someone offered you a smelly old sock? Or maybe the book was right. Anyway, whatever the reason, Rover sniffed at the sock appreciatively and – wonder of wonders – he shut up! Then he picked it up in his teeth and slunk into his crate. With a huge, heart-rending sigh, he flopped down onto his blanket, buried his nose in the sock and shut his eyes.

We looked at each other in stunned disbelief.

'Praise the Lord!' said Dad.

'Uh-oh,' I said, tapping *The Perfect Puppy*. 'God had nothing to do with it this time. It was this book.'

'And whose idea was it to consult that?'

'Nic's.'

Dad raised an eyebrow. 'Depends how you look at it,' he said.

That's typical of my parents. According to them, there's no such thing as a coincidence – well, not in our house, at any rate. If the post arrives on time, it's probably an answer to prayer! The trouble is Mum and Dad seem to do so much praying, it's impossible to work out what's an answer and what isn't! I probably get zapped by one of Mum's prayers every time I come through the front door. There's me, thinking I'm being a nice kind person and making her a cup of coffee, but I'm probably answering her prayer. Or maybe it's the same thing. When I leave home (which'll be soon at the rate we're going), I'm going to do some really objective testing of this praying lark.

Anyway, at least the peevish pooch shut up – and as long as he has a nice fruity pair of Mum's socks to snuggle up with every night, he's fine. There's only one drawback – the sneak raids he makes on the dirty laundry pile when he's feeling lonely.

Anyway, that all seems a lifetime away now. Don't make the mistake of thinking I'm happy about having Rover here – I'm not! And neither is Frisk. As far as we're concerned, he's on probation. One false move and it's back to the dogs' home – even if I have to drag him there myself. No, I'm certainly no happier about the hell-hound but at least he's not as bad as that *witch* Mrs Charmless Peterson.

She's been and gone and done it. Spent hundreds of pounds on Chas's uniform, that is. So there's no going back – even though I went, at great personal cost, and did my nice little middle-class girl act for her. I took flowers. I polished my shoes. I tied my hair back. I even wore a skirt! And then I explained how well Chas was doing at school and how all the teachers like him and how he has loads of terribly nice friends, not just me, and how he *was* going to join the chess club and the debating society and be in the school play which is *bound* to be Shakespeare this year because we did *Grease* last year. I said it all in ever such a nice voice without any slang at all – and I drank gallons of her horrible Earl Grey tea with lemon and didn't make any crumbs with her nasty tasteless Bath Oliver biscuits, but she's *still* going to send him to Saint Poser's School for Posh Kids or whatever it's called.

At least it's something that Mum, Dad and I agree about. Mum went to see her too and Dad had a go at the salon when he'd got her helpless with a highlighting hat on her head – but they had no more luck than me. I can't believe it. Last term was dire because Chas spent most of his time snivelling round after this drip called Cute Carly. This term'll be dire because he won't even be there to snivel! We go back tomorrow. So much for Merry Christmas and a Happy New Year. I think this has been the worst holiday I've ever had.

I can't believe it! Talk about adding insult to injury! We've got a new boy in our tutor group already! And of course, he has to sit in Chas's seat! I can hardly bear to look at him.

I keep forgetting and I glance in his direction thinking I'll see Chas and there's this awful Greg person instead. I'm determined to hate him. He'll have to sit somewhere else when Chas comes back – which he will do, of course. He plans to do so badly at St Poser's that his toffee-nosed mum will just have to let him come home. (It's St Peter's really, but St Poser's suits it much better – you should see the uniform!)

I'm disappointed in Vicky though. She's my best friend – apart from Chas, of course. I never knew she could be so hard-hearted. You should have heard her when we got together at lunchtime.

'Wow, Kate, you have all the luck! You'll have to introduce me to this Greg, you know! All the girls are talking about him. He is *gorgeous*!'

I looked at her as if she'd sprouted an extra head.

'He is? I wouldn't know. Every time I look at him, I think of Chas.'

'Oh, come on, Kate! Don't be so pathetic! It's not as if Chas has died! He's promised to write and he'll be home for weekends sometimes. You're not going to let being all gloomy about him stop you getting to know Greg, are you?'

I was furious. 'You have no feelings, Vicky Dickenson!' I snapped. 'Don't you care that Chas has been forced out of his own home? Don't you care how he's feeling? His term hasn't even started – his chair has barely had a chance to cool down – but it's all "Ooh, isn't Grotty Greg gorgeous? Ooh, smarm, smarm, *please* introduce me, Kate!"'

Vicky laughed. She's very difficult to annoy. 'Oh give it a rest, Kate. You're such a drama queen. Chas is going to be fine – and you *know* he won't forget about you, if that's what's worrying you. Meanwhile, there are other fish in the sea. Gorgeous ones like Greg for example! So let's go fishing!'

I had the sense to simmer down. I'd already lost my best friend for this term. I didn't want to lose Vicky as well.

'Well, it's tough, I'm afraid,' I said, forcing my face into something like a smile. 'I haven't even spoken to him yet. I'll do my best, though, OK? Specially for you.'

Vicky beamed. 'That's more like it! You never know, Kate. You might even like him.'

Huh! Over my dead body!

That was yesterday. What a difference a day makes. Chomp, chomp, chomp. There! That was me, eating my words.

Last night was one of the most embarrassing of my whole life – and I'm an expert! I went round to say goodbye to Chas. The awful thing was that, for once, I couldn't think of anything to say. I was going to stay the whole evening, seeing as we hadn't got much homework, but it was so awkward and miserable that in the end I made up an excuse and said I had to go. That was when things got really dreadful. Chas looked as if he might be going to cry and I had such a hard lump in my throat I could barely speak.

'You will write to me, won't you, Kate?' he said.

''Course.'

'Lots?'

'Yeah, lots.'

'Because I'm really going to miss you.'

I grunted something that should have been 'I'll miss you too' but it didn't come out right.

'I wish we had mobile phones,' said Chas.

I snorted. 'Fat chance of that. Too new-fangled for *your* mum and BDM thinks they fry teenagers' brains.'

'What about e-mail?'

'Only Mum has it. You want her reading everything you send?'

We stood there looking at each other stupidly and then Chas did something that nearly made me keel over and die. He came over, put his arms round me and tried to hug me. I say *tried*, because I was so uptight that I was as stiff as a board and too shocked to hug him back or anything. It was awful – so clumsy and awkward and EMBARRASSING!

'Well, 'bye then, Chas,' I said in this ridiculous little high voice and then I leaped on my bike and tried to pedal away fast. I failed, because of the mud in the farmyard and because I had to open the gate. Chas started to come over to help me but I snapped, 'No, leave it. I'm fine.' I could just see his face in the light from the door – a typical Chas wounded-spaniel look, the sort I usually can't resist. Well, tough! He shouldn't embarrass me like that!

Even so, I still felt a pang every time I glanced over and saw Greg this morning. My cheeks flamed whenever I remembered that last scene with Chas but I couldn't help thinking about what would be happening to him – the journey, the getting there, the meeting new people and so on. I'm afraid my mind wasn't on getting to know Greg at all – and it wasn't on my lessons either.

It was at the end of PSE (that's personal and social education, not perverted sex education as Ben calls it) which we have in our tutor groups, that it happened. My world suddenly changed. Wham! Just like that. You never know when it'll happen, do you?

I was packing my things away when I was suddenly aware that there was someone waiting by my desk. A little shiver ran down my spine because that was what Chas would have done – he was always ready before me. I looked up – and up, even though I'm quite tall myself. Greg is a good bit taller than Chas and broader too.

'Kate?' he said, in this really deep voice. 'Why d'you keep staring at me?'

For a moment, I was dumbstruck. I suddenly realized that Vicky was absolutely right. Why hadn't I seen it before? Grotty Greg was *gorgeous*!

He was smiling at me, obviously in no hurry to go.

'I just wondered,' he said, 'whether you could see some

huge spot on my ear or something? Thought I'd better check.'

'Err… no.' Flustered, I groped for words. 'No… Sorry… I didn't mean to stare. It's just that my best friend used to sit where you're sitting and he's gone away to boarding school today and I just keep thinking…'

I dried up, suddenly horror-stricken to find that if I carried on, there was a very high chance that I was going to burst into tears.

Greg was looking down at me curiously.

'Is he your boyfriend?'

'Oh no,' I gasped hurriedly, astounded to find that now my pulse was racing and I was feeling slightly weak at the knees. Hadn't I had enough breakfast or something? 'No, no. Nothing like that. We're just really good friends.'

'So you're missing him?'

'Yes… well, sort of.'

'Well, I'm missing my old friends too. So we've got something in common.'

He smiled. I smiled back. What now? I've always prided myself on being able to cope with boys. I mean, I'm not bad-looking (even Ben thinks I've got beautiful hair and I'm not too badly off in the bum and boobs department either) and I've just never felt there was much difference between us and them (girls and boys, that is) apart from the obvious. But here I was, almost completely tongue-tied, feeling ready to faint, because a slightly taller, better-looking specimen than average was taking an interest in me. What was going on?

'Do you bring a packed lunch?'

I gave myself a mental shake. 'I'm sorry?'

'D'you bring a packed lunch? Or d'you have school dinners?'

'Oh, school dinners. We're all too busy at home to be bothered making sandwiches. I'm going to meet my friend Vicky...'

I stopped short. This was obviously the moment to take Greg along to meet her – and suddenly, that was the last thing I wanted to do. But it was too late.

'Vicky? Another friend of yours?'

'Yes, we usually have lunch together. Would you like to meet her?' I *forced* the words out of my mouth.

'I'd love to – if she's anything like you.'

That line nearly blew me away. I mean, what on earth are you supposed to say to something like that?

I smiled nervously. 'Come on, then,' I said.

We joined the melee in the corridor and then squeezed our way outside. I was delighted to see that, despite the crush, people were noticing who I was with, especially two girls called Donna and Lisa. They've had it in for me ever since Lisa fell for Chas. So Vicky was right – she wasn't the only one who thought Greg was gorgeous. I couldn't help preening a bit. Across the playground in the lunch queue, I could see Vicky waving excitedly and was just about to take Greg over when I heard my name called. I turned round as slowly as I dared, knowing only too well what I was about to see.

BDM. Of course. Unfortunately, she often pops up at school – doing the odd (very odd) assembly, teaching a bit of RE, being an unpaid school counsellor. Today, as I suddenly remembered, she had come to show off the twins. She and Nic each had a baby strapped to their chests but worse, far, far worse, they had also brought Rover along.

I really didn't know what to do. My first instinct was to storm over and tell BDM to clear off immediately. My second was to pretend I hadn't heard her and hide in the lunch queue. I didn't act fast enough. She was making a beeline for me, with kids falling back to let her through while cooing at either the babies or the dog. Actually, she didn't have much choice. Rover had spotted me and was nearly pulling her arm off.

'Kate, love, I just wondered if you could hang on to Rover while I pop up to the staffroom for half an hour? I know you're about to have lunch but could you eat later?'

Battling hard not to scream at her and fending off Rover at the same time, I said as sweetly as I could, 'Why did you bring him with you, Mum?'

'Oh, you know. He didn't want to be left and it seemed so cruel when he's just settling in. I'm sure he'll be fine with you.'

What could I say? Refuse point blank and make myself

look completely churlish? Or accept half an hour with the hell-hound?

'Oh, all right then,' I grunted, and took the lead – which Rover saw as his cue to jump up and wash my face all over again.

I fully expected Greg to have disappeared into the crowd but no – he was still there, smiling his curious, amused smile.

'So who's this then?' said Mum, panting a little from her exertions with Rover. 'I haven't seen you before.'

'This is Greg,' I said. That was all she needed to hear. I know BDM. Give her an inch, and she'd have Greg's life-story out of him and be offering him a place in the church choir. 'Aren't they expecting you in the staffroom?'

For once, she took the hint. 'Oh, of course. Sorry, Greg. I'm sure I'll see you around. Must dash for now.'

She turned and I was just thinking I'd escaped relatively lightly when she suddenly stooped and fished something out of her bag.

'Oops, sorry, Kate. Nearly forgot. You'd better take this in case he begins to howl.'

And with that, she handed me a very large, lacy white vest. The sort normal girls give up wearing when they're eight.

'Sorry I couldn't find anything smaller,' she said, 'but he should like it. I only had it on yesterday.'

Thank you, BDM! I love you too! I suppose I should just be grateful it wasn't something worse.

3

My Mum Walks
the Dog - Not!

Can you die of embarrassment, d'you think? I mean, really?
I know heart attacks can be caused by bottled-up stress.
Well, being as embarrassed as I was today is certainly very
stressful. And what about yesterday? That awful scene with
Chas! It can't be good for me, it really can't. Whenever
I think over the last twenty-four hours my stomach starts
churning and I start chewing my cheeks. Seriously. Beats
biting my nails, I suppose – at least no one can see what I'm
up to!

Anyway, I reckon my condition is critical. One more
embarrassing episode like tonight's and I'll be foaming at
the mouth and off to the funny farm.

I coped with the vest incident brilliantly, I thought. I just
pretended it hadn't happened.

'Come on, Greg,' I said brightly. 'I'll introduce you to Vicky. Then I guess I'd better take Rover for a walk.'

Despite the fact that Greg couldn't seem to take his eyes off what I hoped looked like an old rag dangling from Rover's mouth (the mad mongrel whisked the vest out of my hand before I could shove it in my bag!), I led him over to Vicky, who was virtually jumping up and down with excitement.

It was a relief to leave Greg with her actually. I did not want to explain my demented family to Greg immediately. Any attempt I might make to prove that I was a perfectly normal girl whom any self-respecting guy might like to befriend was doomed to failure with the dopey dog in tow.

Nonetheless, I wasn't overjoyed with the situation and couldn't believe it when I got home to find that, as predicted, BDM had created a dog-walking rota and it was my turn first.

'Oh, come off it,' I exploded. 'I did my bit at lunchtime. Why can't someone else do it?'

Mum put on her patient look. 'Kate, I've only put you on the rota once a week. I know how you feel about Rover. Your dad, Ben and Nic are all prepared to do two walks a week. And this *has* to be your night. Your dad's got a student night, Nic's got his English class and Ben's got Scouts – so it's down to you, I'm afraid, love.'

'And what about you? Which is your night then?'

'I'm doing all the morning walks. You know how busy I am with the girls in the evening.'

'Busy? Busy? Half the time we help out with bathing them! All you have to do is sit with your feet up and breast-feed them off to sleep! Only you can do that bit, of course! Sounds like a good excuse to skive out of some work to me!'

'Kate, don't be so childish. If you want to entertain the girls while I take Rover out, that's fine by me – but I can't be in two places at once.'

'You wouldn't need to be in two places at once if we didn't have Rover!' I snapped.

'But we do – so are you walking him or not?'

'Oh, I'll walk him then,' I grumbled, 'but I think you're being totally unfair!'

I still do. Normally Mum has a way of backing you into a corner where you know you're wrong and you jolly well ought to apologize but this time... no, she can't be right. No one in their right mind has baby twins and takes on a half-trained dog, no matter how sad the circumstances. It's just too much. I only wish I could find some verse in the Bible that says so and see how she slimes her way round that.

Anyway, I took the demented dog out after tea and that's when the terminal embarrassment really set in.

Although it was dark, it was still early and I knew there'd be loads of people out dog-walking in the park, so I decided to take Rover there. I knew Mr Ponsonby had gone that way sometimes and thought it might make him feel more settled if he saw his old stamping ground.

We managed all right on the way, although Rover did pull terribly. I had to keep changing hands. I resolved to consult *The Perfect Puppy* as soon as I got home to see if it had anything helpful to say about dogs that pull. At this rate, my arms would reach my feet by Easter. Very attractive – not!

It was when we got to the park that the trouble really began. We walked through the car park, Rover sniffed the air excitedly and then – whumph! He took off with such a start that I completely lost hold of his lead!

'Rover!' I shouted. 'Rover! Come back!'

He didn't even pause. Within seconds, despite me haring after him, he had disappeared, a black dog, invisible in the black night.

Now what? I stopped running and stood, panting, trying to collect my thoughts. Should I keep on shouting? Should I search the park in a systematic way? Should I run back home and get help? What? What on earth do you do if you lose your dog? Call the police? Organize a search party? I had no idea.

I looked around frantically. Every other dog I could see was either walking calmly on his lead or bounding around within a short distance of his owner. Should I stop someone and ask for advice? Knowing my luck, anyone I asked would turn out to be the mad axe man and it'd be bits of me being sniffed out of some ditch next morning by a man and his DOG!

I made a decision. I was not going home without Rover.

That would just look too pathetic – or worse, Mum might even think I'd lost him deliberately. Tempting, I know, but I'm not that big a rat.

So what next?

'Rover?' I shouted tentatively. Then louder, 'Rover!'

That was the thing to do, I thought. The park isn't huge and there are old-fashioned street-lamps lining the paths. I'd just have to search it carefully and keep shouting. Embarrassing but necessary.

A man with a huge, scruffy-looking animal that could have been a small horse smiled as I passed him in the glow from a lamp.

'Don't worry, love,' he said. 'He'll come back when he's hungry.'

Very encouraging. Rover had had his tea just before we set out. I'd be there all night!

I wiped my sleeve across my face. I was not going to cry. A delinquent dog was not going to get the better of me. I was jolly well going to find him – the only problem was how.

I was just pausing to think through my next move when it began to rain – real slushy winter rain that could almost have been snow. Brilliant. My first attempt at walking the dog and I began to think that walking on fire might be more fun – and worse was still to come.

I pulled up my hood and pushed my hair out of my eyes. Every dog-walker in sight seemed to be whistling or calling and walking rapidly towards the exit. It wouldn't be long before I was alone in the park in the dark in a slush storm. Oh joy! It was getting increasingly difficult to see much at all but suddenly, in the distance, I thought I could see a dark shape bounding towards me.

'Rover!' I shouted joyfully. 'Here, boy! Good dog, Rover!'

But it wasn't Rover. As it got closer, I could see it was a much bigger and hairier animal than him. What on earth could it be? I began to back away. In the dim light shed by the street lamp, it looked like some sort of bear – or perhaps a very shaggy lion. And then, as if that wasn't bad enough, I realized that what I'd taken to be its shadow was another creature, exactly the same!

I admit it, I panicked. Ours is one of those parts of the country where, every so often, some innocent rambler sights some curious creature or some picnicker finds he's put his flask down in a very strange footprint. And now it looked like it was my turn to meet the Beasts of Banbury.

My determination to find Rover vanished. Whatever was chasing me could jolly well eat him instead. I raced back along the path, my one thought to get as far as the car park where I might at least find someone to help. Better the mad axe man than the Banbury Beasts!

It was wet, it was dark, my hair kept falling into my eyes and I was in a blind panic. So I didn't see the person walking towards me until – crack! – I ran straight into him just on the bend by the little humpback bridge which crosses the stream that feeds the pond. The next second

I had slipped in the slush and was slithering down the bank into the water.

It's not very deep just there – just squelchy and smelly – but it was bad enough. It was even worse clawing my way back up the bank and finding that the bloke holding out his hand to help me up was none other than Greg Barker! Why me? Why is it *always* me that this sort of thing happens to?

'Kate?' he said, in disbelief. 'Is that you?'

But at that moment, out of the corner of my eye, I saw that the beasts were upon us.

'Quick!' I shrieked. 'They're going to get us!'

I turned to run but Greg grabbed my shoulders.

'Kate, what on earth's the matter? Are you scared of big dogs or something?'

'They're not dogs, they're…' I stopped. The beasts were panting at Greg's side while he clipped their leads in place.

'No… I… no… I thought…' I got no further. I just wanted to throw myself back in the pond and bury myself in the stinking sludge.

It was obvious now that my wild beasts were dogs. Huge and very hairy, but dogs nonetheless.

Greg was laughing. 'Kate, what are you like?' he said. 'Did you think they'd escaped from a zoo? They're Newfoundlands. This is Chloe and this huge chap is Biggles. I guess they would look pretty fearsome if you weren't expecting them.'

'It was dark,' I said feebly, 'and I was in a bit of a flap.'

Really, I just wanted to go home as fast as I possibly could. My stomach seemed to have shrivelled into a hard little knot with embarrassment, I was cold, my feet were wet and I was very aware of the revolting stagnant smell seeping up my body – but I still had to find Rover.

'Why?' said Greg. 'What's the problem?'

I explained.

'But haven't you got some sort of call he'll recognize? Some whistle or signal that he understands?'

I shook my head. 'We only got him yesterday. It's the first time I've taken him out.'

I knew exactly what he was thinking – that I must be a complete idiot – but, watching his immaculately behaved dogs waiting patiently beside him, I knew I had to swallow my pride and ask his help. I gulped and… a minor miracle occurred.

Bounding down the path, looking very pleased with himself, came Rover. He shied away when he saw me and would have darted off again but Greg was too quick for him – he shot out a hand and grabbed his trailing lead.

'Yours, I believe,' he said with a grin and handed it over. 'Now keep tight hold of it this time!'

I didn't reply, just wrapped the lead several times round my wrist before Rover began to drag me off in the direction of home.

Greg hurried after me, with Chloe and Biggles walking calmly to heel.

'You ought to take him to dog-training classes, you know,' he said.

'I'm sure we should,' I said, trying not to snap, 'but we've got rather a lot of other stuff to cope with at home.'

'Just an hour a week would be a start,' he said. 'Honestly. And then you can practise when you're out with him.'

'You seem to know a lot about it,' I said, tight-lipped.

'Well, I ought to. My parents are dog trainers. That's why we moved here. They've bought some old kennels and they're doing them up. It started as a hobby but they've gone professional – they do training, breeding, kennels – the lot. And I'm helping with some of the classes. Shall I book you into one, d'you think? We've got some spaces in one of the Monday evening classes. That should suit Rover.'

My brain was reeling. Two days ago, I would have cheerfully eaten slugs rather than go to a dog-training class, but having just been publicly humiliated by the horrendous hound and with the prospect of an hour a week with Greg tempting me, I couldn't resist.

'Yes, please,' I said, trying not to sound too eager. 'Well, that's if it doesn't cost too much.'

'It'll be money well spent. I'll get my mum to ring yours. What's your number?'

I told him. He repeated it several times while we walked to the car park.

'Well,' I said regretfully, 'Rover's certainly keen to be off. I have to go this way.'

'Really? So do I,' said Greg. 'I'll walk you home.'

I couldn't believe it. Did he really want to walk home with me – someone who didn't know a Newfoundland dog from a grizzly bear and who, right now, smelled like a bog?

Somehow I managed to string a few words together as we walked along the street, though I was panting with the effort of trying to hold Rover back to Chloe and Biggles' sedate pace. Greg chatted genially about his dogs and how he'd trained them up and begun to show them. His family don't just watch Crufts – they take part! If I want to improve his opinion of me, I'd better learn to tell my bulldogs from my boxers pretty quickly.

'Well, here we are,' I said when we reached our gate. 'I'll be seeing you then.'

'Oh, I might as well just pop in and tell your parents about the dog-training…'

No, no, no, I thought frantically, imagining the dog-crate in the hall festooned with nappies and the babies doing their bath-time bawl.

'Oh, don't worry,' I said brightly. 'I can explain it. I'll see you tomorrow!'

Then I bolted up the garden path before he had a chance to argue.

Ten minutes later, I'd peeled off my stinking socks, shoes and trousers and had donned my dressing gown while I waited for a bath. The girls were in full cry and I was *very* glad I hadn't let Greg in. Dreamily, I sat in front of my dressing table and brushed my hair. He must like me, I thought. To have walked me home after seeing what an idiot I was. He must really like me. Walking Rover suddenly seemed much more attractive than helping bath babies in the evening – because presumably Greg had to walk Chloe and Biggles every night too.

I'd just dreamed up a scene in which we took a romantic springtime walk with three impeccably behaved dogs when I was rudely interrupted.

'I saw who you came home with, you jammy so-and-so,' said Ben. 'How did you manage that, then, Miss Boys-don't-interest-me-Lofthouse? Vicky is going to be green with envy. Or aren't you going to tell her?'

'Shut up and go away, little brother,' I said, in what I hoped was an offhand voice. 'It's none of your business.'

'Ooh, hoity-toity! I seem to remember it was very much *your* business when I started going out with Suzie.'

'That's because you were nothing more than a baby and needed someone to keep an eye on you.'

'Oh, and you're maturity itself then, are you? Not!'

'Oh, go away, Ben. I only met him yesterday. He only walked me back from the park. He's just a friend.'

'Oh yes,' said Ben. 'That must be why you're gazing into the mirror admiring yourself then. Who are you trying to kid? You've got the hots for Greg Barker – it's obvious. You never sat gazing into the mirror when you'd been out with Chas.'

Chas! Hearing his name was like a sudden cold shower. I gasped.

'Chas! I must write to him! I'd forgotten…'

'All about him?' Ben finished for me. He raised an eyebrow.

'No! Don't be stupid, Ben. He's my best friend.'

There was an odd silence. My words seemed to hang in the air.

Ben was right. From the moment I'd left Greg with Vicky at lunchtime, I hadn't given Chas a thought.

4

My Mum and the Dog Class

There are some people who always fall on their feet. You know the sort. They always crawl in just after the bell but the one day your teacher decides to slam everyone in detention for being late, they're away with the flu. Or you go on a school trip and they forget their sandwiches. Any other person would get bawled out and left to scrounge leftovers from their friends – but the teacher lends *them* some money for fish and chips.

Well, I'm not that sort. I'm the sort that falls on my bum – and I usually land in something soft and smelly. I get the detentions and the leftovers.

This journal is proof.

Dog-training classes. With Greg. Also with Rover. Bit of a drawback but never mind. I spent the weekend daydreaming about it. Mum had booked us in. It was all arranged. Vicky had ground her teeth and was being a bit sniffy with me but apart from that there wasn't a cloud on the horizon. I'd even had a letter from Chas – rather embarrassing really, mostly about how much he was missing me – but I scribbled a quick reply and put it out of my mind. I mean, life goes on. What with the dog to train and all the homework I'm getting, not to mention the usual chaos in this house, I can't be writing pages and pages. I'm sure he'll be OK once he settles in and he'll soon be home for a weekend.

It was Monday morning when BDM dropped her bombshell.

'Don't hang around after school, will you, Kate?' she said. 'We'll have to be very quick off the mark if we're going to get everyone fed before we go to this dog class.'

'Oh, it's not far, Mum,' I said. 'I won't need a lift.'

'I wasn't offering you one. You're right. We can walk.'

The penny dropped.

'You're not coming too, are you?' I demanded, totally horror-stricken.

She looked blank. 'Well, of course I am. I'm Rover's pack-leader. I'll have to practise what he learns while you're at school. But I'm really pleased that you're coming too. Two heads are better than one. I knew you'd get to like Rover once he'd settled in.'

Ben took one look at my face and choked on his toast. Seriously. Nic thumped him hard on the back while shovelling mashed banana into Comet and said tactlessly, 'What's wrong, Kate? Don't you want Jo to go?'

'Um… no… I mean yes, that's fine… sorry, I just feel a bit queasy – must have eaten my breakfast too quickly.'

'Kate, what *is* the matter with you?' demanded Mum. 'You've been gazing into space with that slice of toast in your hand for a good ten minutes! Aren't you well? Or have you gone off the idea of these classes? I can go on my own, of course, but I thought you wanted to come.'

'Of course I want to come,' I said, pulling myself together quickly. 'I was just thinking about what a rush it'll be for you. What will you do with Hayley and Comet?'

'Oh, they'll be fine till we get back – as long as we don't hang around afterwards.'

Great! Bang went my dream of a leisurely walk home with Greg, Chloe and Biggles – oh, and Rover. Brilliant! With a mum like mine, who needs enemies?

When I got to school, Vicky was no comfort, of course. In fact, she clearly found it hard not to laugh. Ever since I'd told her about the classes, she'd been wondering how she could beg, borrow or steal a likely looking hound to take along. She would have split her sides if she could have witnessed the scene when BDM and I finally arrived – late, of course – at the kennels.

I took one look inside the training hall and nearly turned on my heel and fled.

It wasn't the dogs that were the problem, although there

47

were certainly far too many for my taste, most of them yapping their heads off. It was something else entirely – the fact that virtually all the other dog owners were young and female!

Reluctantly, I followed Mum in. Despite the noise, the class had obviously begun as everyone was grouped in a large circle, their dogs more or less at their feet. So all eyes turned in our direction. They usually do. BDM always attracts attention. Today we had Rover as well and – just my luck – he was the biggest dog there and the loudest. Clearly completely over-excited, he pulled on his lead, desperate to get away and sniff some bottoms. (Question: why do dogs have to greet each other with a nose stuck in each other's privates? Gross or what? I mean, it's bad enough for us humans when we have to do the polite peck-on-the-powdery-cheek with Great-Aunt Gertrude!)

It was all so overwhelming that it took me a few moments to work out that actually, there weren't very many dogs or owners there – but that two of the owners were the people I'd least want to meet anywhere, let alone at a dog-training class with Greg. They were:

a) Chas's ex-girlfriend whom we've always called Cute Carly because she's one of those precious princesses who does nothing but ballet and nail-polishing.

And worse:

b) Lisa, who holds it against me that Chas won't go out with her.

They only need to work out that they *both* hate me and I'm – guess what? Dog meat.

Their dogs suited them. Carly's was a small and yappy poodle – what else? Lisa's was one of those ferret-faced mongrels – eyes too close together, muzzle too long, lip too curled. Yuk. Made me feel quite warm towards poor old Rover. At least he *looks* nice!

Anyway, I'd only had a chance for a quick glance round when a woman in smart jeans and a sweatshirt called us to order.

'Greg will be bringing round some treats for the dogs,' she said. 'Use them to keep your dog lying down while I explain what we'll be doing. In future, can you ensure that you come with your own supply of your dog's favourite treats please.'

Carly put up her hand. 'Excuse me,' she said. 'I've brought Sadie's favourite treats tonight. Shall I use those?'

Sadie! I ask you! I suppose I should be grateful that Mr Ponsonby didn't choose a worse name for Rover.

'Yes, of course,' said the woman, whom I assumed was Greg's mum. 'That would be excellent, Carly.'

Carly looked smug and I pretended to vomit into my hand.

'Behave!' hissed Mum. 'I'm having enough trouble with Rover! Talk to him or something, can't you?'

Rover, who, seconds before, had been lying down nuzzling Mum's hand in a surprisingly submissive manner, was now struggling to get up.

'What's the matter with him?' I said. 'Where are the treats?'

'He's scoffing them too quickly!' said Mum. 'I've hardly got any left and she hasn't explained anything yet! Well, look at him! He's twice the size of any other dog here!'

I leaned heavily on Rover's haunches while Mum broke off a tiny bit of whatever it was she'd been given. Great! We were making a fine impression. We hadn't even started and I was having to virtually wrestle Rover to the floor.

'Now,' announced Greg's mum, 'since this is the first class, the dogs are going to be very excited and...'

Too right! Completely frustrated, Rover gave a great heave and launched himself at Mum's chest.

'Aagh!' yelled Mum, falling over backwards, the remains of the treats showering out around her.

Pandemonium! Every dog made a bolt for them. The next few minutes were a horrible confusion of barking, trailing leads and shouting owners, while the dogs demolished the treats and then did their best to demolish each other.

A wild glance around as I helped Mum haul on Rover's lead told me that unlike his mother, who was in the midst of the fray trying to help, Greg was doubled up with laughter at the side of the ring. Great! The only consolation was that if he was laughing at me, he was probably laughing at Cute Carly and Lousy Lisa too.

At long last, we all had our dogs back, now even more excited than ever. Rover still seemed to be sniffing round hopefully for more treats. Well, that's what I thought at the time.

'Don't worry at all,' said Greg's mum, though her smile looked a little strained. 'They all need to get to know one another. Greg will bring round some more treats and we'll try…'

Her words trailed off as Rover, with an air of huge cheerfulness, made a large puddle on the floor.

'Oh gosh, I'm terribly sorry,' said BDM brightly. 'I forgot to take him before we came in.'

'That's quite all right,' said Greg's mum, her smile even more strained. 'We expect the occasional accident. Greg, the mop please.'

Greg came over with a mop and bucket. I don't know whether he was smiling or frowning because I couldn't look. To be so humiliated in front of Cute Carly and Lousy Lisa and him – it was too much! I plunged my face down to meet Rover's and pretended we were having a heart-to-heart about his bladder problem. Actually, if I'd said anything at all, I would have burst out crying. I was extremely glad of Rover's big, shaggy head to hide in and of my own mass of hair, which after the wrestle and the scuffle, probably didn't look much different from his.

'I don't understand it,' said Mum as Rover produced yet another gallon of wee in the yard outside, after a further half hour of torture. 'I mean, he did do something as we walked here, didn't he?'

I didn't care. So Rover peed a lot. Well, maybe dogs did. They just had to learn to do it in the right place – and that was not in front of my worst enemies and the boy I thought I might be in love with. I could still see him, inside the hall, chatting to Carly and Lisa. He'd smiled at me once in the whole hour and hadn't spoken at all. OK, so he was busy – but still.

'Come on, Rover, you canine catastrophe,' said BDM cheerfully. 'Come on, Kate. Don't look so glum. He wasn't so bad after that first bit.'

Wasn't so bad? Ha! Who was she trying to kid? Compared with the prissy poodle and the foxy ferret-face, he was a complete deviant!

'I know what you're thinking, Kate,' said BDM, 'but he really isn't as stupid as you think. Look, he's not pulling as much already.'

'That's just because he's exhausted,' I said cruelly. 'And so am I.'

'Oh ye of little faith,' said BDM.

'It's nothing to do with faith,' I snarled. 'That dog is a moron.'

Rover glanced over his shoulder mournfully.

'He heard you,' said BDM.

'Don't be ridiculous. You'll be saying he understands every word we say next!'

'Not at all. I'd just prefer you not to insult him.'

'He's a dog, Mum! D-O-G dog!'

'You still don't need to be foul-mouthed. God didn't give us animals to abuse.'

'I wasn't abusing him, I was just…'

'I think you've said enough, Kate. Do I take it you're not coming next week then?'

I thought about it. Another hour of ritual humiliation in front of Cute Carly, Lousy Lisa and Gorgeous Greg. And then I thought of Lisa and Carly sucking up to Greg with their cutesy-yucky little doggies in tow.

'No,' I said, setting my jaw. 'I'll give it another go.'

'That's more like it,' said BDM. 'Faint heart never won fair lady – and it probably applies to drop-dead gorgeous boys like Greg too.'

'Is that a quote from the Bible?' I snarled.

'No, but it ought to be,' she said. 'Which reminds me, Kate. Have you written to Chas yet?'

Honestly! My mother. Sometimes you'd think she'd lose her head if it was loose but really she doesn't miss a thing.

5

My Mum at the Petersons

I've just had a huge row with Mum. It ended with her sending me up here – to write to Chas! So I'm typing away at this journal instead. What an interfering old bat she is! I shall write to Chas when I jolly well want to, not when she says so. It's not as if I haven't written – I have – just not as much as he (or she!) would like me to. That's what the row was about. He sent her a postcard. 'He sounds really lonely,' she said, reading about a hundred words between every line. 'When did you last write to him, Kate?'

That's how it started. Two minutes later I was being accused of laziness, selfishness, wilful neglect, disloyalty and goodness knows what other crimes – all because the wretched woman thinks I'm so besotted with Greg that I've forgotten all about Chas! 'Open rebuke is better than hidden love,' she said in this oh-so-wise voice. 'Think about it, Kate!' Puke! One of her handy little quotes from the Bible. She may be on maternity leave but she certainly hasn't forgotten she's a part-time vicar! The cheek of it! It wasn't much more than a year ago that she was acting like some sort of medieval Lord of the Manor, virtually locking me into a chastity belt because I was spending too much time with *Chas*!

I told her what I thought in no uncertain terms. Mistake. So here I am, *not* writing to Chas!

The trouble is… well, actually I don't know what the trouble is. I've never felt like this before. I just can't seem to settle to anything. All my get-up-and-go seems to have got-up-and-gone! BDM had a real go at me for being moody too. Well, I suppose I am. I certainly don't feel very happy. Not like I used to. Even when BDM was at her irritating worst and even when I was panicking about the twins being born, there were times when I know I felt really, really happy. Now I seem to feel pretty gloomy most of the time. Is that what being in love does to you? Is that what it is? Am I really in love? If so, I think it's overrated. Oh, I know it's fantastic when Greg smiles at me or talks to me – my heart starts to pound and I feel on top of the world – but it doesn't last. I suppose that's why people who are in love want to be together so much – so that crazy, thrilling roller-coaster feeling can go on for ever. But then how d'you get anything else done? Call me unromantic but let's face it, life has to go on, doesn't it?

Vicky isn't much help at the moment. She seems just as moody as I am. She's not at all happy about me being as mad on Greg as she is – especially as I get to go to Rover's classes with him. Maybe I should ask Ben about it. I mean, presumably he's in love with Suzie – they've been together for months now and they seem happy enough. I feel a bit stupid asking my little brother about these things... but hey, who's going to know?

I tracked Ben down easily enough. He was plugged into both his computer and his personal CD player. Tragic waste of human brainpower. I had to practically disembowel him to get him to listen.

I went straight for the jugular.

'Are you in love with Suzie?'

'Dunno.'

'What d'you mean, dunno? *How* long have you been going out with her?'

'Dunno.'

'Ben! Wake up! Don't you care about her at all? Is she just a habit?'

Ben looked puzzled. 'A habit? What? Like picking your nose?'

'Ben! Be serious! What d'you feel about Suzie?'

'I really fancy her.'

'You are *so* shallow.'

'Well, you did ask.'

'Is that all then? Don't you feel anything else? Heart pounding, weak at the knees, breathless, butterflies in your stomach – that sort of thing?'

''Course I do. Like I said, I really fancy her. You're very thick, Kate.'

'No, I'm not. That isn't fancying someone, is it? That's being in love.'

Ben shook his head. 'Nah. If you're in love, it's like she's your best friend in all the world – *and* you really fancy her. Just fancying someone isn't being in love.'

'So is that how you feel about Suzie?'

'Hmmm…' Ben scratched his chin thoughtfully. 'Yeah, I think maybe I do. That's sorted, then. I must be in love with Suzie. Happy now?'

I threw a pillow at him. 'No, you great idiot. I don't want to know whether *you're* in love with Suzie…'

'You don't? I thought…'

'NO, you gormless nerd! I'm trying to work out if I'm in love with Greg!'

'Oh, that's easy.'

'It is?'

'Yup. You're not.'

For a moment, I was speechless. Then…

'How would *you* know?' I demanded.

'If you don't think I know, why are you bothering to ask me?'

Sometimes my little brother is even more irritating than

BDM. I sucked in my cheeks to stop myself swearing at him.

'OK then,' I said dangerously. 'So how do I feel about Greg, Mr Know-it-all?'

'Oh, the same as every other girl in your year. You just fancy him.'

That was when I scragged him. He's bigger than me but I'm fitter and I was really angry. When I'd got him pinned to the floor and begging for mercy, I said, 'Don't you dare say that about me, ever, ever again, all right? Got that, you spineless lump of blubber?'

'All right,' panted Ben. 'Can I say something else though?'

'What?'

He reached out for a postcard that was lying on the floor under his desk.

'When did you last write to Chas?'

Mercy? I don't know the meaning of the word!

That was a week ago. Now I consider myself to be a fair and reasonable person. I did not dismiss Ben's comments totally out of hand, despite their rather unsophisticated nature. I have known others turn to Agony-Uncle Ben for advice on their love life – Chas, for example. But where has it got me? Not very far. Except – and it's a fairly big except – I'm pretty darned sure I'm not in love with Chas Peterson, nor ever will be. According to Ben's definition, that is. In fact, I'm not even sure he's my best friend in the whole world any more. I can't believe a few weeks at boarding school could have changed him so much! Maybe it's his hormones.

We were invited to the Petersons' for lunch. Chas was home for the weekend. We usually go on a Sunday, but according to Mrs Charming, Chas was so keen to see us all that she wanted us there on Saturday. At least that meant we were spared taking Granny who always spends Sunday with us, though these days she whiles away most of the time snoring peacefully. The same can't be said of Rover, who had come with us, despite my protests.

'Don't be so mean, Kate,' said BDM. 'He'll love it up at the farm, and if we leave him he'll be on his own for hours and hours. And he's behaving much better now. We can show off how much he's learned.'

It's certainly true that Rover is improving. He must be settling in all right because he's given up his dirty laundry fetish. Thank goodness for that! I kept worrying that one day he'd mistake my clothes for Mum's (I mean you can't expect a dog to tell the difference between size 8 and size 18, can you?) and somehow I didn't fancy wearing mine after they'd been wrapped round Rover's nose! Our Monday evenings of torture are having some effect too, even if they're not progressing my friendship with Greg. He has at least spoken to me the last couple of times and is as friendly as ever in school but there's been no suggestion of another walk with Chloe and Biggles – and I *always* see Cute Carly and Lousy Lisa chatting him up at the end of class. Ben's right about that bit anyway – *all* the girls in my year really do seem to fancy him. Maybe that's why he hasn't bothered with me as much as he did that first couple of days – there're too many other fish in the sea. But I can't quite believe he didn't think there was *something* special about me, for a little while, at least.

Anyway, I was still excited about seeing Chas. What with feeling so confused about Greg and with Vicky being so peculiar with me, I was really looking forward to seeing his friendly face. And, secretly, I wanted to put Rover through his paces and impress the Petersons. I haven't forgotten that Chas's mum thinks I'm not the sort of girl Chas should be mixing with. Well, I can't do dressage for the pony club, but at least I could show her a few tricks with a dog!

Things didn't start too badly – with Rover, anyway. I had him on his lead when we arrived as Mum was busy with the babies and I was ready for him when he made to jump up at Mrs Charming.

'Off, Rover,' I said firmly. 'Off!'

Maybe he was nervous, maybe it was the tone of my voice – whatever it was, he thought better of jumping up and just pulled on his lead a bit instead.

'Good boy, Rover,' I said, quickly shoving a doggie treat in his mouth. 'Now, sit!'

And he sat! I swelled with pride. There! Maybe Rover

wasn't such a moronic mutt after all – or maybe I'm a better trainer than I thought I was. That's what I imagined at the time, anyway. Well, guess what it says in the Bible? 'Pride comes before a fall.' BDM told me that later. Very comforting – not! I thought part-time vicars were supposed to be tactful – even if they *are* on maternity leave.

Anyway, so far, so good. Rover was over the threshold without having completely disgraced himself and was enjoying oodles of attention. So were the babies. Mrs Charming couldn't decide who to coo over most. I was so busy showing off Rover, who was still sitting quietly as good as gold, that it took me a few minutes to look round for Chas.

He was leaning against the newel post at the foot of the stairs, his arms folded.

'Hello, Kate,' he said coolly when he met my glance.

'Stay, Rover,' I said, letting go of his lead and taking a couple of steps away from the hubbub at the front door.

'Hello, Chas,' I said. Suddenly, I didn't know what on earth to say. I was remembering that awful, embarrassing goodbye scene and I found I couldn't meet his eyes. I mean, what if he tried to hug me again now? Confused, I turned back to the dog and grabbed his lead.

'Mum,' I said. 'Shouldn't I take him outside for a minute? We forgot to let him – you know… (I found I couldn't say what I meant in front of Mr and Mrs Charming) … when he got out of the car.'

'Gosh, yes, Kate – take him out, quickly. Sorry, I should have thought.'

I hauled Rover out – he wasn't impressed – and bingo! he soon sniffed out a spot to produce a gigantic puddle. I breathed a huge sigh of relief. We still hadn't sussed why Rover produced such gallons of wee and I couldn't help feeling a bit smug that I'd averted a carpet catastrophe.

Dad met us in the hall as we came back in.

'Lunch won't be ready for a while,' he said. 'Why don't you and Chas try and wear Rover out a bit beforehand? Then he might sleep while we eat.'

It was a good idea. We've been putting Rover in his crate while we eat at home but we couldn't fit it in the car with all the baby clutter as well. The last thing Mrs Charming would want was a hungry hound marauding round her dining table and I was very keen for him to keep up the good impression he'd made so far. The only problem was – Chas. He had looked so glum – not like the Chas I used to know at all. I wished Ben was with us. He was joining us later but had been invited to lunch at Suzie's first. I could drag Nic out with us but I knew that would only make things more awkward. Chas has been funny about the fact that our au pair is male ever since he arrived. So I was stuck. Rover, Chas and me it would have to be.

'Wait here,' said Dad. 'Chas'll be out in a minute.'

I waited, whiling away the time practising a few 'sits' and 'downs' with Rover. We were fast discovering that he'd do almost anything for food and I had loads of dog treats in my pocket.

'Very impressive,' said a voice behind me.

I spun round. 'Chas!' I said. 'You made me jump!'

He shrugged. 'I came round from the side door. Nothing unusual in that, is there?'

'No, no, I...'

'You were busy with your dog.'

It hung in the air like an accusation.

'Yes,' I said. 'Yes, well, he does keep us very busy.'

'I guessed.'

Silence. I didn't know how to break it. What on earth had happened to him? He was supposed to be dying to see us – so why was he being so grumpy? I crouched to fuss Rover, unsure what to do.

'Come on, then. Are we going for a walk or not?' He made it sound like an invitation to join him in the electric chair.

'Of course,' I said, as brightly as I could manage. If I jollied him along, surely he would snap out of it? And Mum calls *me* moody!

'So,' I tried, as we crossed the yard, 'how's it going then?'

He gave me a hard look. 'Haven't you got my letters, Kate? Or haven't you bothered to read them?'

'Of course I've read them,' I said, firing up. 'But you can't expect me to remember every single word. Anyway

I want to know more. All the stuff you *haven't* written to me about.'

'There isn't much else to say. It's just as bad as I expected. Worse, actually. I expected you to write more.'

'I've written lots!' I protested. 'I've just been very busy, what with the dog and everything. You know I've been going to these training classes and... oh bother... I shouldn't be letting him pull on his lead like this. Sorry, I'll have to concentrate on him more.'

It was hopeless. I simply couldn't talk to Chas properly and coax him out of his absolutely foul mood *and* get Rover to do what he should at the same time. The moment I stopped encouraging Rover to walk to heel, he would lurch ahead and drag me along at a trot – and I couldn't let him off the lead because of all the livestock about.

Chas tramped after me in silence, glowering down at his boots.

'Look,' I said at last, in exasperation. 'Let's stop at the gate. I'll tie Rover to it and then we can talk properly, OK?'

For a split second, I saw a glimmer of a smile pass over Chas's face – and then fate, or whatever it is that makes proud people fall, took a hand.

Someone was out shooting rabbits. Rover heard the first shot and panicked. I was just threading his lead through the gate when he lurched away from me and the next moment, for the second time in less than a month, I was empty-handed and Rover was haring away at a pace I couldn't possibly hope to match.

'B*****!' I exclaimed.

'Too right!' said Chas, for the first time sounding vaguely like himself. 'The sheep are about to lamb. Will he bother them, d'you think?'

'I don't know!' I howled. 'He's not really used to them. Come on – we'll just have to go and see!'

We weren't in open fields but there were endless gaps in the hedge where a determined dog could wriggle through and get among the sheep. I had no idea whether Rover would want to do that or not.

Suddenly, an awful thought grabbed me. I lurched to a stop.

'Chas!' I panted. 'Whoever it is that's out with a gun… if Rover goes in with the sheep, would they…?' I couldn't say it. Rover is a real pain but I didn't want him shot dead for worrying sheep.

''Fraid they might,' gasped Chas. 'Come on!'

We pounded back on down the hill, eyes peeled for a blob of black in the distance. It was awful but at least Chas and I were on the same side again.

Before long, I couldn't run any further. I doubled over, panting, crippled by a bad stitch. Chas ground to a halt beside me.

'It's no good, Kate. We'll never catch him,' he said breathlessly, leaning on my shoulder. 'We'll just have to hope he's gone straight back to the farm. At least I can't hear any sheep – if he was in with them they'd be making an awful row.'

Chas was right. I stood up and smiled at him gratefully. For a moment, my friend was back. Then he looked away.

We walked on as quickly as we could, too breathless to speak. Imagine my relief when we strode into the yard and Rover came bounding to meet us, his mouth wide open in a welcoming grin. I knew there was no point in being horrible to him – he wouldn't make the connection – but I couldn't help being distinctly cool as I picked up his trailing lead.

'We'd better take him round the side,' said Chas. 'You'll need to clean him up a bit.'

Chas was right. The track had been wet and muddy and it looked as though Rover had bounded through the worst of the puddles on his mad charge home. His lead was sopping wet and covered in goodness knows what, so I unclipped it and hung it from one of the pegs inside the door. Why did I do that? Why? Aagh!

Chas chucked me an old towel and left me to it. I'd always thought he quite liked dogs but he clearly didn't want to spend any more time than he had to with Rover. I didn't blame him. Rover was not at all happy with the idea of being rubbed down and my attempts quickly degenerated into a kind of all-in wrestling match. I was fed up, I was hungry and my temper was getting frayed. I'm ashamed to say I took it out on Rover. His belly and legs were going to be clean and dry if it was the last thing I did. I wish it had been. Suddenly, with one massive, determined squirm, Rover wrenched himself free and was off, skidding across the hall, barging through the sitting-room door and running amok among the coffee tables.

Pandemonium! I was after him as fast as I could but not before he had cleared a coffee table of its books and flowers with one excited sweep of his tail. The babies were bawling and Rover was alternately jumping up or dodging whenever any of the appalled grown-ups tried to grab him. Why, oh why had I taken off his lead? There were muddy paw-prints on the beige carpet and several coffee-cups had been launched across the room. If this carried on, there would be complete carnage!

I stood still and put my hands on my hips. 'Rover!' I bellowed at the top of my voice. 'Rover! Sit!'

Rover stopped. He looked at me. To my amazement, he slumped down on his haunches.

'Well done, Kate…' started Dad, always my best supporter, but he spoke too soon. The next moment Rover was on his feet again and throwing up violently all over the hearthrug.

We all stood transfixed, gazing in horror at the mound of oozy whitish sludge which Rover had produced.

Dad was the first to speak. 'What on earth has that dog been eating?' he said, expressing all our thoughts.

Chas chose that moment to reappear. In his hand he had

a large cake-plate. On it were the remains of what had obviously been a very spectacular raspberry pavlova.

'I found this on the floor of the utility room,' he said.

Mrs Charming rose to the occasion admirably. 'Silly me,' she said, in a kind of strangled squeak. 'It's not his fault. I should never have left it where he could get it. Poor Rover – he didn't mean any harm.'

6

My Mum and Gran

I forgave Mrs Charming a lot that day. She was adamant that it was no one's fault but her own, despite the fact that if I hadn't let go of Rover (twice) he would never have found his way into the utility room or the sitting room. She packed Chas, Nic and me off to the snug to entertain Hayley and Comet, while she and the rest of the adults cleaned up the mess.

'I've got an apple pie in the freezer we can defrost,' she said brightly. 'No one's going to starve!'

As if that was a problem! Rover's artwork on the hearthrug had probably put everyone off their lunch! But Mrs Charming enjoys a crisis. Really, she's missed her vocation. Prime minister would be right up her street.

Sadly, we're not all as forgiving as she is. I'm not, for one. I felt so humiliated I simply wanted to crawl into a hole and die. Instead, I was on entertaining baby duty. Hungry baby duty. Nic was busy rocking Comet and singing in her ear;

I was stuck with Hayley and was simply not in the mood for a quick burst of cheery baby rhymes. She grouched and grumbled on my knee while I scowled at Chas who promptly turned on the computer.

'Oh, I see,' I hissed. 'You're just going to leave Nic and me to struggle with these two, are you? When you were the one who must have left the side door open!'

'We always leave the side door open in the daytime,' said Chas, without turning round. 'Give it a rest, Kate. It's just one of those things. So your pooch isn't perfect. It's not the end of the world. If anyone should be upset, it's Mum.'

Nic looked up from Comet. He must have seen that I was close to tears.

'I think you could be a bit more nice, Chas,' he said. 'Kate is very upset by all this.'

I groaned inside. Nic meant it kindly – he's the gentle giant sort – but it was a disaster. Chas spun round on his chair just as Nic was giving me a reassuring squeeze.

'I know she's upset,' he snapped, 'and I really don't know why. Nobody's blaming her or her stupid dog. She's just in a foul mood and has been since the moment she got here – it's quite obvious she never wanted to come in the first place!'

And with that, he stood up, slammed his chair into the computer desk and stormed out.

I limped through the rest of the day. Rover, well and truly worn out, slept for hours and the grown-ups had a high old time telling sick stories. Just what I needed – you know – which child/dog/cat had been sick where and on what. Ha, ha, very funny – not! Ben turned up mid-afternoon and was very happy to join Chas, locked into some mindless computer game. Which left Nic and me. Somehow he didn't seem as vastly entertained by the sick stories as the others.

'Shall we go for a walk?' he suggested. 'The babies are asleep.'

'A walk?' I said. 'Without either the babies or a dog?' I smiled tiredly.

'We can talk. It is good for my English.'

I am normally very careful around Nic. He's nineteen, tall, quite good-looking – and French. I've learned from experience that Chas feels a bit threatened by him – even though I've told him there's no way Nic could ever be such a good friend as he is. But today? Well, I didn't care. It looked as if my friendship with Chas was in tatters anyway. If Nic wanted to practise his English on me, then so he should.

We set out at a brisk pace. I'm not used to being on my own with Nic and was just wondering what to say when he launched in.

'Kate, you need to be careful with Chas,' he said.

I stared at him in surprise.

'Careful?' I said. 'What d'you mean? I thought…'

'I know – he was being horrible to you – but it is because he is so miserable.'

71

'Miserable? At his school, you mean?'

'It is not just his school. He is miserable about you.'

'About me? But he's acting like he'd rather I wasn't here!'

'That is because he has come home and all you do is with the dog.'

'Rover? But that's not true! I mean, I never even wanted a dog! It's just that now that we've got him and I'm helping with his training – well, I mean, he needs a lot of time and attention and…'

'And actually, you quite like it.'

'No – well, yes – I mean no…' I stopped. Nic was right. I *did* quite like it. There was a real satisfaction in getting Rover to do what I said. Despite the aftermath, that moment when he'd stopped charging round the sitting room because I'd told him to – well, I'd felt a huge surge of pride.

Nic smiled at me. 'It is fine, Kate. Lots of people like training dogs. But do not forget about Chas. He needs you and he is – how do you say? – jealous, jealous of the dog.'

'Jealous? Of Rover? Don't be ridiculous, Nic. You must mean something else. You can't be jealous of a *dog*!'

Nic shrugged. 'I think you can, Kate. I think Chas is. Just think about it. OK?'

I changed the subject quickly – and I am *not* going to think about it even though I said I would. Frankly, I think Nic is being over-dramatic. I mean – jealous of a dog that pukes over your mother's best rug? Give me a break! It probably comes of being French – too romantic, if you ask me. There's certainly something funny about Chas but it's definitely not that – probably just hormones and school. Anyway, I'm not going to worry about it. I'm sure he'll settle down. I get moody – he gets moody. What's the big deal? Let's hope he's feeling better by tomorrow.

All that seems like years ago. I came home from school on Monday to disaster. Nic was alone with the babies and fretting about what to feed us – he may be French but his cooking is more beans-on-toast than cod-on-blur. (Question: what on earth is cod-on-blur anyway? Another weird French delicacy like frogs' legs or snails? I must remember to ask him sometime. And I bet I've spelled it wrong.)

'Nic, stop fussing,' I said firmly. 'Tell me what's going on, will you? We won't starve – there's a chip shop down the road. Where's Mum?'

'You should sit down, Kate,' said Nic sombrely. 'It is bad news.'

'What's bad news?' demanded Ben, bursting through the back door at that moment. 'If it's that no one's been shopping, I'm out of here. I'm starving. I'll go and scrounge some grub off Suzie.'

'Ben, please be serious,' said Nic, as earnestly as he could, considering that Comet was trying to stick her fingers up his nose. 'Your mum and dad have gone to the hospital. Your gran was rushed there this afternoon. They think she may not…' He stopped, obviously finding it difficult to finish what he had to say.

'Last much longer?' suggested Ben nervously. He had gone a ghastly white which made all his freckles stand out.

Nic nodded. 'Survive the night, I think they said.'

Ben and I looked at each other. Gran had been in a nursing home for some time now and hadn't been herself since a nasty bout of pneumonia, but the idea that she might die – our barmy but still feisty grandmother – well, it didn't bear thinking about.

'What happened?' I asked, a catch in my voice.

'I am not sure,' said Nic. 'I am sorry. I only know we have to find something to eat, bath the babies and get them ready for bed. Your mum is coming home for their bedtime but will go back to the hospital once they are asleep.'

It's strange how at times like this, the most trivial things suddenly seem tremendously important.

'But what about Rover?' I said, suddenly realizing he wasn't there.

'He is in his crate. I could not cope with him *and* the babies.'

'No, I mean, it's his training class tonight – what about that?'

'Oh, go on your own if you're that worried, Kate,' snorted Ben. 'As if it mattered just for once – but I suppose you don't want to miss seeing the Boy Wonder, do you? Get your priorities right, hey Kate? Gran's dying but you can't miss out on Gorgeous Greg!'

'Don't be so horrible, Ben,' I retorted, rounding on him. 'I wasn't thinking of that at all. I just wondered what Mum would want me to do – and really, I might as well go. I can't do anything to help, just sitting here twiddling my thumbs.'

'You could pray.' Ben looked pious.

'Of course I'll pray, you moron! Don't go all super-spiritual on me – it doesn't suit you! And I can pray all the time I'm walking there and all the time I'm walking back.' Over the last year or so, I've prayed in some pretty funny places, I can tell you – hospital loos, beaches, trains, graveyards… I didn't need Ben pretending I had to kneel down at the foot of my bed or something.

'Unless Gorgeous Greg walks you home,' Ben persisted.

'Oh yeah, right! Give me a break, will you? He barely even speaks to me these days!'

'So you say.'

'Yes, so I say. What's got into you, Ben? Who rattled your cage?'

And then Ben started to snivel and scrubbed one eye with his fist. Suddenly I realized what was really wrong and what a cow I was being.

'Oh Ben,' I said and put my arm round his shoulders. 'I'm sorry. Come on, Gran's a real old trooper, you know she is. It's probably just a false alarm. I'm sure she'll pull through.' I nodded at Nic who had a packet of chocolate digestives in his hand and a question mark on his face.

'Come on, we'll have a drink and a biscuit and then I'll ring the hospital to see if we can get any news, all right?'

Ben nodded and blew his nose hard. 'I don't need a biscuit,' he mumbled. 'I'm not a little kid. I'll just ring Suzie.' He stumbled out into the hall.

'Oh dear,' I said. 'Shall I take Rover or not? Will you be all right on your own, Nic?'

'I will be fine. It will be much better if you are both busy. Waiting is hard.'

I knew Nic was talking sense, so as soon as we'd eaten our fish and chips, I set off with Rover. That was when it really hit me. Gran – mad old Gran, the cause of some of my most excruciatingly embarrassing moments – might not still be here in the morning.

It doesn't matter, does it? Someone can be a real pain half the time, but you can still love them. I love Gran. I remember what fun she was before she got really old and ill. I remember all the times she slipped me fifty pence when I was desperately saving up for something, and the endless games of snap or snakes and ladders she used to play with us on wet Sunday mornings when Mum was frantically running round getting ready for church. Even now, I love listening to her singing all her funny little rhymes to the babies and waiting for those moments of real sanity when she'll put Mum or Dad firmly in their place. Only yesterday, BDM was trying – and failing – to impress her by taking Rover through his paces.

'For heaven's sake, leave the poor animal alone, Jo,' she said. 'He's a pet – not a contestant for "One Man and his Dog", though I must say, in that outfit, you'd fit in rather well.'

'Oh,' said BDM, looking crestfallen. 'I rather like this casual look.'

'It's fine for shepherds,' said Gran. 'You're not one.'

You're left feeling so helpless after a put-down like that, because there's no point in defending yourself. Next moment the mist will have come down, and she'll think you're some filmstar or other.

But I didn't want her to die – not for a good long while yet – and as I made my way to Rover's class, I couldn't help tears rolling silently down my face. I tried to pray but I wasn't sure what to pray for. After all, Gran *is* very old. Maybe it isn't fair to try to hang on to her – especially if heaven is as good as it's supposed to be. As we turned into the kennels, I stopped for a moment to try to pull myself together. Don't be stupid, I told myself. She isn't dead yet! I blew my nose noisily.

'Kate?'

Greg was walking down the yard towards me, a sack of dog biscuits over his shoulder. Why, oh why, did he have to see me like this? I drew back into the darkness a little, scrubbed at my face and shook my hair forwards.

'Kate? Is that you?' Rover was whining and dragging me towards Greg; he could hear the other dogs gathered in the training barn. The security lights made me screw up my eyes; I knew it must be obvious I'd been crying.

'Kate, what's happened? You've been crying! Where's your mum?'

Greg put the sack down and looked at me intently. His unexpected warmth was too much for me. I promptly burst into a full-blown howl. Somehow he worked out what had happened from my garbled explanation.

'Kate, that's awful! Look, let me just tell Mum – I'll walk you back home.'

'No, no,' I protested. 'I want Rover to do his class. He's been doing so well and he likes it so much. I'll be all right – really. I'm being silly – she's not dead yet.'

'We-e-e-ll,' said Greg. 'If you're sure. Look, I'll take you to the house. You can wash your face and…'

'Pull myself together?' I gave him what I hoped was a brave smile.

He grinned. 'Yes – you'll only miss a few minutes. Come on then – just don't mind the dogs, all right?'

I heard them before I saw them – a huge, deep barking greeted us as we opened the gate. Once through the front door of the cottage, I had to push my way through a heaving mass of excited fur to get to the cloakroom.

'Were Chloe and Biggles in there somewhere?' I asked afterwards as I unfastened Rover who'd been going nearly demented outside.

Greg laughed. 'Couldn't you recognize them?' he said.

I shook my head. 'I don't even know how many dogs there were, never mind which was which!'

'There were only six, actually. But you can meet Chloe and Biggles again afterwards when I walk you home.'

'There's really no need…' I stammered. 'I'll be all right, honestly.'

Greg shook his head. 'I'm not so sure. You've had a nasty shock. And anyway, it'll be a pleasure.'

I felt as if I'd grown a good ten centimetres. I floated into the training barn, beyond caring that Rover was barking fit to bust and that everyone was staring at us. Let them stare, I thought. One in the eye for you, Cute Carly and you too, Lousy Lisa. No chatting up Greg tonight – he'll be walking home with me!

That walk! Will I ever forget it? It wasn't very easy to talk because I had to work hard at keeping Rover walking to heel but Greg was all encouragement. He seemed to think we were doing really well. When he could, he told me all about training Chloe and Biggles. At our gate, he made them sit quietly while he said goodnight.

'Don't worry about your Gran, Kate,' he said. 'I'm sure she'll be fine.'

And at that moment, so did I. With a boy like Greg to be my friend, or maybe even my boyfriend, anything seemed possible.

I came back to earth with a thud when I opened the

front door. Mum was feeding the babies and Nic told me she was going back to the hospital as soon as she could – Gran's condition was still critical. Ben had gone round to Suzie's. Nic made me a hot chocolate and oozed sympathy but I suddenly felt overcome with tiredness. I suppose the emotional upheaval of the last few hours had worn me out. I picked up my mug and was just on my way upstairs for a relaxing bath where I fully intended to spend a nice, lazy time daydreaming about Greg when the phone rang.

'The hospital!' I exclaimed and sprang to pick it up, spilling my drink en route.

'Kate?' The voice at the other end was familiar but I suppose I was in such a state I couldn't recognize it.

'I'm sorry, I...'

'Come on, Kate! It's me – Chas!'

'Chas! I'm sorry! I wasn't expecting you – I thought it was the hospital – you see, Gran...'

'I know. That's why I'm ringing. Mum rang me. She thought I should know.'

'But how did *she* know?'

'Nic has to call her if there're any problems he can't deal with overnight.'

'Oh – I see. But...'

'So how is she?'

'Still critical.'

'Oh.'

Silence. I didn't know what to say. If he'd been home, if

things had been how they used to be, I'd have been round at his house on a night like this or he'd have been here. But things have changed so much. My mind was full of Greg's ready sympathy and, as I held the silent receiver, I became increasingly irritated with Chas. Couldn't he think of even one comforting remark? Even something obvious like, 'It'll seem better in the morning' would be better than nothing.

'Kate...' he said at last, his voice sounding a bit odd. 'Are you still there?'

'Of course I'm still here,' I said crossly. 'Is that all you rang for?'

'Yes... no... well, look, I'm sorry, Kate. And I'm praying for her, OK?'

'Thanks. Well, if you don't mind, I'll go now. I'm really tired, all right?'

'Yes, of course. Sorry. Well, 'bye then, Kate. Let me know how she gets on.'

'OK. 'Bye then.'

''Bye.'

It was hard not to slam down the phone. He was so useless! Fancy bothering to phone if he couldn't think of anything helpful to say.

'Honestly!' I said, glaring at Nic, who was watching me from the kitchen. 'What *is* the matter with Chas these days? If that was supposed to be sympathy, I don't think much of it.'

Nic shrugged. 'Chas is fond of your Gran,' he said. 'It must be hard for him not being here.'

'Well, he could make a bit more effort!' I snarled. 'What's the point of ringing me if he can't manage to say anything?'

'Actions speak louder than words,' said Nic. 'It is one of your English proverbs. It is in one of my textbooks.'

'Well, right now, I'd rather listen to Greg's *words*,' I snapped. 'At least he made me feel better not worse! And don't you start quoting things at me please – it's bad enough having Mum forever ramming bits of the Bible down my throat!'

Nic smiled and shrugged. 'Sorry I spoke,' he said.

Urgh! Why do I have to live with the founder members of the Chas Peterson fan club? If it isn't one of them nagging me about him, it's another. Well, right now, I'm starting a Greg Barker fan club and I'm going to be his number one fan! So there!

7

My Mum and the Disco

Gran survived. The acute kidney failure that sent her hurtling into hospital miraculously got better by the morning.

'Never seen anything like it,' said the doctor, shrugging.

'That's what prayer's all about,' said Mum smugly.

Well, perhaps she's right but it does puzzle me how sometimes prayers seem to work and sometimes they don't. I mean, take my situation with Greg. Actually, I'd rather not take my situation with Greg, I'd rather make snowballs in hell – but I know from past experience that writing about the worst embarrassments of my life does actually help, so here I am back at the jolly old computer. The point is, though, I do keep praying about Greg – not that he'll ask me out or anything silly like that (well, not much anyway) – more that if he doesn't care about me,

I could stop wishing that he did. Doesn't seem much to ask, does it? But nothing happens. One minute Greg really seems to like me (like on that blissful walk home the other night) and the next minute I'm just any old girl! Either way, I feel ill!

The night that Gran went into hospital, I thought we'd shared something really special – but the next day it was almost as if it had never happened. Oh, he was perfectly pleasant and friendly to me – just as he is to any reasonably pretty girl. But no more than that. Maybe I'm expecting too much. I mean, until I met Chas and Vicky, I didn't really have any very special friends – I just got along pretty well with everyone. And he hasn't been here very long. Perhaps he's just testing the waters – except – except... well, it's just that he's been so specially nice to me twice now that... well, I just wonder, that's all.

Huh! So much for that theory! I'm so worked up I'm surprised my fingers aren't melting this keyboard! I'm incandescent – now there's a good word. After last night, it's quite obvious that there's *somebody* he really likes – and it certainly isn't me! So why do I still care?

Last night we had a Year 9 Valentine's disco at school. I have to admit, I went along feeling really excited. Vicky came over to my house and we spent simply ages getting ready. I never used to bother much about what I wore but I knew that Cute Carly and Lousy Lisa would dress to kill and I didn't want to be totally outdone. I'd even managed to scrounge a new outfit out of BDM and, to Dad's amazement, I'd asked him if he could do my hair. I didn't want him chopping chunks out of it so he put some fancy gel stuff on and then blow-dried it for *hours*! By the time he'd finished, I looked as if I'd stepped straight out of a shampoo advert – you know, all swirling, glossy tresses. All I needed was a sickly smile to go with it. Anyway, the boys seemed to like the effect.

I met Ben in the hall.

'Nic!' he shouted. 'Nic! Are you expecting someone?'

Nic stuck his head over the banister. 'No. Why?' He looked at me and pulled a puzzled face. 'Who is this then? Someone for you?'

'Oh shut up, you idiots,' I said, flattered nonetheless. 'You know it's me!'

Ben gave me a friendly shove.

'Hey, watch my dress!' I said. 'And my hair!'

Ben groaned. 'Hey Nic!' he called up. 'We're in trouble now, you know.'

'Why?'

'Kate's finally turned into a real girl. There'll be no room for our stuff in the bathroom soon and we'll never be able to get near the phone. Oh, and she'll probably start eating nothing but salad. Shame really. I rather liked the old Kate.'

'Ben! Don't be ridiculous! I'm not going to turn into Cute Carly or someone!'

'So you say,' he said gloomily, and went upstairs whistling the funeral march. Honestly! Brothers!

Anyway, Vicky was thrilled with what Dad did with her hair too and we set off for the disco in great spirits. Vicky seemed to have forgiven me for liking Greg. After all, I was hardly the only one. I'd half-expected Mum to give me a lecture on the beauty of the inner self – she has a good Bible quote about that – but for once I was spared, thank goodness. She and Dad are a bit preoccupied at the moment – still worried about Gran. I'm afraid I haven't given her much thought, now she's better. I've had other things to worry about.

Secretly, there was another reason I was excited about the disco. Something had happened which I hadn't told anyone about. I had received a Valentine.

I'd been lying in wait for the postman, just in case, and could hardly believe it when, along with the handful for Ben (how does he do it?), there was an envelope for me. I checked the postmark carefully. It was local. Then I sneaked it up to my room. My heart was racing as I opened it. Surely, surely that must mean I really was in love, whatever Ben said?

It was a very tasteful card – white with a simple design of hearts and roses. Inside was printed, 'For someone special'. There was nothing else. No handwritten message, no kisses or signature. But I could think of only one person who could possibly have sent it. Greg. What *would* he do at the disco?

We arrived to find the usual scene – girls giggling in groups, boys huddling together looking as if their arms and legs didn't quite fit. Nobody dancing.

'I'm just going to check my hair,' said Vicky and waltzed off before I could stop her, leaving me feeling as if I'd suddenly been stripped naked. I could see several people, both boys and girls, staring at me and began to wonder if I ought to go and check myself over too – maybe I had a huge rip in the back of my skirt or something. Just as I'd decided I couldn't stand it any longer, Greg strolled in through the door and walked straight over to me.

'Wow, Kate, you look fantastic,' he said. 'I hope you're going to dance with me later.'

I took a deep breath. 'What's wrong with now?' I said. 'Somebody's got to get things going.'

'What? On our own?'

'Why not?' I said bravely. I'd already worked out that neither Cute Carly nor Lousy Lisa nor (and this was a bit mean) Vicky had finished in the loos yet, and I was enjoying imagining their faces when they walked in to find me already dancing with Greg.

Greg shrugged. 'Well, OK then. After you.'

It wasn't a great moment, that moment when I had to bite the bullet and do what I'd just suggested. Don't worry, I told myself. Once you get going so will loads of others. Bolstered by the thought of getting one over on Carly and Lisa, I strode out into the middle of the hall.

Loads of others *didn't* join us. For a few ghastly seconds I thought no one would at all – but then a few did and then a few more and by halfway through the track I was actually beginning to relax. Predictably, Greg was a good dancer and seemed to be enjoying the fact that he was virtually the only boy on the floor. People were definitely staring at us but I'd stopped worrying about what I looked like; they were probably just staring at Greg.

The next song had just started and I was beginning to feel quite high, what with knowing I looked good and dancing with the best-looking boy in my year, when my eyes strayed across to the door, searching for Carly and Lisa. Instead I spotted two completely different people, one of whom was the very last person I wanted to see.

My heart sank. There could be only one possible reason that my appallingly embarrassing mother was here. Gran must have had a relapse. And behind BDM, closely followed by Vicky was – Chas!

'Excuse me,' I shouted at Greg above the music. 'I have to go for a minute.'

He nodded and followed me politely.

'What's the matter?' I demanded, as soon as I'd reached Mum. 'Is it Gran? Is she…'

'Oh no, Kate. No. Oh, I'm sorry if I worried you. No, your Gran is fine – it's Mr Clarke who isn't.'

'Mr Clarke?'

'You know – one of your teachers. He's gone down with

88

the flu and can't make it. They didn't have enough adults here – so they rang me!'

I couldn't believe it. It's been rather nice while BDM's been on maternity leave. She hasn't kept popping up at school doing assemblies or RE lessons, but the staff obviously haven't forgotten her. Oh no. She's far too useful as general dogsbody and last port in a storm, worse luck.

'Why didn't you say "no"?' I snarled. 'Couldn't they have found someone else?'

'Kate, don't be churlish!' retorted Mum. 'The babies are asleep, I'm free – why should I refuse? The school needed me.'

'Because… because… oh never mind!' I spluttered and turned on my heel, completely forgetting that Chas was hovering close by. Honestly! I think BDM was *born* middle-aged! I mean, how was I supposed to strut my funky stuff with *her* hanging around watching – and what about all those slow numbers at the end? How was I going to *smooch* with *my mother* watching?

'Er… Kate?'

'What?' I snapped at the unfortunate boy I'd just barged into.

'Er… would you like to dance?'

'What?' I demanded. 'Are you serious?' The boy, a perfectly nice chap from my Maths set, looked distinctly nervous.

'Yes… of course… well… er… *would* you like to dance with me?'

'I'm sorry, I…' I looked round for Greg. He had gone. I searched the group by the door. No. By the drinks and nibbles? No. With mounting horror, I scanned the dance-floor. There he was. Dancing his little heart out. With Cute Carly.

I grabbed the boy's arm quickly, so hard that he yelped. 'Yes,' I said fiercely. 'Yes, of course I'll dance with you. I'd love to. Right now.'

After that, it was madness. I'd barely shaken off one partner before another seemed to be queuing up. Every so often, I glanced round to check on Vicky but she seemed to be fine. First she was chatting to Chas, then she was having a drink with him and finally they were dancing together. I could only assume that Vicky had invited Chas. I certainly hadn't told him about the disco. They seemed happy enough. Happier than me, anyway. It was very flattering to have all these boys wanting to dance with me but why hadn't Greg asked me again? He seemed to be splitting his attention between Cute Carly and Lousy Lisa. So what was wrong with *me*?

I had just come to the miserable conclusion that he couldn't possibly have sent me the Valentine and that, given the number of boys asking me to dance, it could be from just about anyone, when something happened that made me want to kick out all the disco lights. BDM started to dance! With our head of year. I had been so furious I hadn't noticed before but she was wearing what she clearly thought was suitable disco kit. She's lost weight since she had the twins but her bum would still cover two seats on the bus and the rest of her has a distinct tendency to quiver. Urgh. Not a pretty sight on the dance floor – especially in her gold and black striped Ali Baba pants and her T-shirt that read 'Bop till you drop' in silver lettering.

'Excuse me,' I said to the hapless boy I was dancing with. 'I've just got to go and sort something out!'

I stomped over to BDM.

'What do you think you're doing?' I hissed in her ear.

'What does it look like, Kate?'

'Stop it! You're embarrassing me!'

'Why?'

What could I say? 'You can't dance and you look awful?'

'You just are!'

'Well, I'm not standing around getting bored all evening. Just pretend I'm not here.'

'How can I when you're making such an exhibition of yourself?'

BDM broke into a peal of laughter. 'You're a fine one to talk,' she retorted breathlessly, obviously determined not to stop dancing, 'wearing that dress and dancing with absolutely anyone who asks you! You've danced with more boys tonight than I've had hot dinners! Don't you think you should sit out for a bit and give someone else a chance? And don't you think you should at least *speak* to Chas?'

Chas! Chas! She always seems to drag everything back to Chas.

'He's perfectly happy with Vicky.'

BDM raised her eyebrows. 'Whatever you say, Kate. Now go away, do. You're cramping my style.'

Huh! I was cramping *her* style! Who did she think this disco was for? I stomped off, head down and barged straight into Chas.

'Sorry,' I said, without looking up, making for the girls' loos.

'Is that it for tonight then? Sorry?'

I stopped but I was too cross to be pleasant.

'What are *you* doing here?' I demanded.

'Same as you, I expect. Trying to have a good time. Vicky invited me.'

'Oh… I see…' Same old problem. I just didn't seem to know what to say to Chas any more. 'Well, what are you waiting for?' I blurted when the silence had become awkward. 'Are you going to ask me to dance or not?'

'Not if you don't want me to.'

'I never said that! You are impossible – I just *asked* you! Would I bother to *ask* if I didn't want you to?'

'You didn't ask me to dance. You asked if I was going to ask *you* to dance. Well, demanded, actually. And you didn't sound very keen.'

'Oh, does it matter? What d'you want me to say? Is this better? "Oh Chas, please will you do me the honour of dancing with me? You are the only fit partner for me!"'

'Clearly I'm not,' said Chas, in a voice that could have iced over the Mediterranean. He turned on his heel.

It was only then, too late (as usual), that I realized how foul I'd been.

'Chas!' I called after him. 'Chas!' But if he heard me, he didn't respond and I wasn't going to go grovelling. In any case, he had walked straight over to Lousy Lisa and the next moment was dancing with her. She tossed me a smug smile and I was left, for the first time that evening, without a partner.

I got myself a drink and sipped it slowly. Vicky was dancing with a boy at least a head shorter than her. BDM was dancing with the *caretaker*! For crying out loud, he must be old enough to be her father! And Greg? Greg was dancing with Cute Carly – but for some reason, that seemed the least of my woes. I didn't feel like dancing any more but, even so, it was a huge relief when a tall boy who plays badminton for the county asked me to be his partner. At least it kept me busy.

The rest of the evening was torture. Greg seemed to be spending more and more time with Cute Carly, BDM started on a charitable mission to get all the geeks and the creeps on the dance floor and, now that he'd got started, Chas seemed to have absolutely no shortage of partners – in fact, girls seemed to be queuing up for him. Absence makes the heart grow fonder or something – I can't remember anyone apart from Lousy Lisa taking much interest in him *before* he went to boarding school.

It must have been about half past ten when I suddenly realized I hadn't seen Vicky for a while and felt a bit guilty. Where was she? I pushed my way through the crush and checked the loos.

'Have you seen Vicky?' I asked a girl who was redoing her mascara.

'I think she's gone outside.'

'What? *With* someone?' I demanded, shocked.

'No. I think she was crying.'

'Crying? Why?'

'Dunno. She's *your* friend. Go and see.'

I hurried out, feeling terrible. I'd been so busy pretending to enjoy myself that I hadn't spoken to Vicky for hours – and now she was *crying*. What on earth could have happened? I just hoped she hadn't decided to go home on her own. Her parents would be furious.

I had to look carefully in the dark outside. I didn't want to disturb any couples. By the time I found Vicky, I was wishing I'd grabbed my coat. It was bitterly cold and she was huddled up beside one of the huge wheelie bins – not the most pleasant place to squat down in my glad rags.

'Vicky!' I said. 'What are you doing out here? It's freezing!'

She didn't say anything.

'Come on, Vicky. What's up? Aren't you enjoying the disco?'

I detected a slight shake of her head.

'But why? You look fantastic! And you seemed to be having a great time with Chas!'

'I was *not* having a great time with Chas! I could hardly get a word out of him! Might as well go to a disco with a pile of wet washing!'

'But you invited him!'

Silence.

'Didn't he want to come?'

More silence. Then…

'Of course he wanted to come. He just didn't want to be stuck with *me* all evening!'

'Well, he isn't stuck with you now – he's dancing with anything that moves. I don't get it. Why does that mean *you* have to be out here crying? You don't fancy him, do you?'

'Of course I don't! You know who *I* fancy! But he obviously doesn't fancy *me*! He hasn't asked me to dance once!'

'Oh, I see.' I searched frantically for something comforting to say.

'He danced with *you!* Well, he danced with virtually everyone except me – and now he's stuck with that awful Carly. And I haven't got *anyone* decent to dance with – now that Chas has given up hanging around waiting for *you*!'

'Don't be stupid. Chas hasn't been waiting for me. When I asked him to dance, he wouldn't.'

'Huh!' Vicky virtually spat at me.

'What d'you mean, "huh"?'

'I mean you are so incredibly dense, Kate. He spent half the evening hanging around with me, waiting for a gap in your hectic social schedule and then when it came, you were foul to him! Of course he doesn't want to dance with you *now*!'

'That's ridiculous, Vicky! He's having a great time! I am absolutely fed up with people going on and on at me about Chas. It's not my fault if he chooses to be so funny with me.'

'Yes, it is! You're his best friend. Or you were!'

'Well, I'm not any more! He's changed too much.'

'It's not him that's changed, you disloyal cow, it's you! Ever since you set eyes on Gorgeous Gregory, you couldn't care less about poor old Chas!'

I was angry now. Really angry. 'That's not true! Ever since he went to that stupid school, he's been horrible to me. You should have seen him when we went round to lunch. Cold and snooty and sneery about Rover...'

'You see! It *is* you! A few weeks ago, you hated the thought of that dog! Now, just because Grotty Greg is dog-mad, you're all doggy-soggy too! I'm not surprised Chas feels left out! You're so ungrateful, Kate. If I had just *one* decent boy asking me to dance tonight because he really wanted to, I'd be over the moon. You've had half the year queuing up for you *and* you've got Chas who really cares about you and you can't even see it!'

'That's because it isn't true! Honestly, Vicky, I don't know why but since he left home he's changed so much we can hardly even speak to each other!'

'It's *you* who's changed, Kate. You, you, you!'

'Stop saying that! It isn't true.'

'Oh go away, Kate. Just go away and leave me alone.' Vicky stood up. 'I'm going home. Don't bother to call me – I'll see you on Monday.'

'Vicky, you can't just go! Mum's giving you a lift! Your parents'll go mad. *She'll* go mad. Please don't go!'

But already she was walking away. 'I don't care,' she said. 'Just leave me alone, will you?'

I suddenly realized that I was absolutely freezing. Until that moment, I'd been too agitated to notice but it would be madness to follow her without my coat. I ran back into the school to find Mum.

There are *some* good things about Mum. One is that she's quite good in a crisis. She didn't ask awkward questions, just got out her mobile and went off to phone Vicky's parents.

'It's all right,' she said, when she'd returned. 'Her dad will drive out to meet her. Now, d'you want to tell me what it was all about?'

'No,' I said and burst into tears.

8

My Mum and I Fight!

This has been one of the most horrible Mondays of my life – and I've had lots. First of all, Vicky wouldn't speak to me – well, hardly. We've never had a row before and I didn't know what to do. I thought of saying sorry – well, sneaky sorry, as Ben would call it. That means saying this really lovey-dovey, flowery sorry that you don't really mean, just to smooth things over. He's brilliant at it. Fools Mum every time and it's excellent on teachers.

'Ben Lofthouse! Why isn't your shirt tucked in?'

'Oh, isn't it, Miss? Oh, I'm terribly sorry. I must have forgotten.'

'Well, don't let it happen again.'

'No, Miss, of course not. I'm ever so sorry.'

Teacher smiles at this charming, apologetic pupil and goes off for cup of coffee. Ben goes round the next corner and pulls his shirt out again. Doesn't work quite so well on men though, especially not on Dad.

Anyway, I'm not such a good actor as Ben and somehow I can't be quite so two-faced with my friends. And I really don't think I've got anything to be sorry for. I mean, is it my fault if all the boys ask me to dance? Or if Chas chooses to be miserable about me? Anyway, I don't believe he is – not for one moment.

Mum thinks it's my fault though. I got a lecture once I was home. I'd sneaked off to my room, pretending I'd got loads of homework to do before dog-training but really I felt too miserable to be a jolly baby-minder before tea. Then Mum came and trapped me. The quiet talk in your room is always bad news especially when she begins it with, 'Now, I've said it before and I'll say it again, Kate – "Open rebuke is better than hidden love" – I'm only going to say this because I really care about you…'

It's at that point that you wish you could close your ears like a camel but God didn't include that in our design-spec, worse luck.

Anyway, this time it was yet another little gripe about Chas – how she'd been thinking about it and he really had looked miserable at the disco and even worse at church yesterday and why hadn't I stayed to speak to him after the service and wasn't I friends with him any more? Then she gave me this really tacky greetings card with this bit from the Bible all written out in fancy writing, all about LOVE.

'Love is patient, love is kind, it does not envy, it does not boast, it is not proud, it is not rude…' honestly, it goes on and on and on. You'd be perfect if you could manage all that. And it doesn't say anything about a pounding heart or feeling weak at the knees – but I still don't think that's just fancying someone.

I'm not sure what her point is. Last year Dad kept on at me that 'a friend loves at all times'. So maybe Mum means I should 'love' Chas even though he's being such an idiot. But what if he isn't my friend any more? Or maybe it's something to do with Greg, like if I really love him, I should be *pleased* he's found Carly? That's about as easy as being *pleased* if Gran dies because she's going to heaven. Well, I don't know – I'm fed up with the whole lot of them – Vicky, Chas, Greg, Mum. I can see why some people prefer animals.

Take Rover, for example. I just have to feed him, take him for the odd walk and play a few games with him and he adores me! Much easier – even if he is a bit smelly. Even the wee problem seems to have sorted itself out – the vet thought it was over-excitement. Doesn't surprise me – I mean, one minute he's living with this dear old gentleman and the highlight of his life is chewing slippers, the next minute, he has his own private entertainment troupe, complete with cut-throat cat to get his adrenalin going.

Take all that back! All sympathy for Rover has officially finished! I've just discovered that the witless woofer has chewed up one of my new trainers!

'It's because he loves you – well your smell, anyway,' said BDM, as if that helps. 'It's quite flattering really.' Of course he hasn't made such a good job of it that she'll buy me new ones. No such luck. According to Mum's jolly little list, love 'keeps no score of wrongs'! Well, sorry, Rover, in that case, I certainly don't love you because there's no forgiveness for this – never, ever, ever! Brand new trainers! You don't deserve to be taken to dog-training classes, you ungrateful hound!

I wish I hadn't gone. I nearly didn't, what with Rover chewing my trainer and with the thought of watching Cute Carly and Gooey Greg gazing across the training barn at each other – puke! I can't believe he's been taken in by that prissy little thing but it certainly looked that way at school today. Well, Chas got tired of her before very long – let's hope Greg does too. Surely, surely someone as kind and friendly and sensitive as Greg can't see much in someone like her – all tutus and poodles? For goodness' sake, what would she say if one of his huge dogs jumped up at her? 'Ooh, ooh, watch my lipstick!'? 'Course they won't jump up though, will they? Too well trained. Pity – otherwise her poxy little poodle might make a tasty snack for them. (Question: why do people clip their poodles into such weird shapes? If they like bare bottoms, why not just get a baboon and have done with it? Seems a shame to do it to a dog.)

Anyway, I did go to the class. I didn't want to give Cute Carly the satisfaction of thinking she was the reason

I wasn't there. I wish I hadn't bothered.

First mistake, we got there early. I don't know how we managed that. Our clock must be wrong. Instead of making our usual dramatic entry, we had to gather with the ordinary mortals and mutts outside the barn and wait. Rover didn't seem himself at all – very quiet and not at all interested in the other dogs.

'Look, Kate, isn't Rover being good?' said BDM. 'He's learning really fast.'

I wasn't so sure. I thought he had a kind of sad, uncomfortable look.

Anyway, I didn't have long to think about it. Just then Lousy Lisa arrived, hauled along by her rat-fink. I was pleased to see how little the ferret-faced mongrel seemed to have learned.

'Hiya, Katie,' she said. (I hate being called Katie and she knows it.) 'I didn't see you dancing with Chas the other night. Aren't you friends any more?'

I was just trying to think of a really cutting reply when Mum answered for me.

'Of course they're still friends,' she said. 'Far too good to need to hog each other all night.'

Thank you, Mother. You have your uses.

'I know that's not strictly true,' she muttered, turning her back on Lisa. 'But I can't bear the way that girl's always trying to dig the knife in.'

'Thanks,' I whispered and then we had to go into the barn.

I had thought I would have to spend the whole hour trying not to throw up over the doting lovers. Actually, they were the least of my worries. There was definitely something wrong with Rover.

For a start, he didn't want to go into the barn. He normally can't wait to bound in and start barking his head off. When we'd finally coaxed him in with most of the treats we'd got for the whole hour, he slumped down on the ground and looked woebegone.

'He's probably just tired,' said Mum. 'We managed to get him out for quite a run in the park this afternoon.'

The trouble is, Mum's already had one embarrassing encounter with the vet. She took Rover along because he seemed hot and floppy – the vet maintained that she'd probably overstimulated him.

'Dogs are not children, Mrs Lofthouse,' he'd said. 'They do not need to be constantly entertained. This one is still growing. Try letting him sleep more.'

She didn't take kindly to being told that, as you can imagine.

'Overstimulated – rubbish!' she chuntered, when she got home. 'I bet he's the sort of man who leaves his dog home alone all day and thinks that stimulation is telling him to bring his slippers. He ought to be reported to the RSPCA.'

'Mum, he's a vet,' I said. 'Is he likely to be into abusing animals?'

'Doctors do,' she retorted.

'What, abuse animals?' I said.

'No, abuse their patients. Sometimes they even murder them.'

And with that remark, she stomped off to sort out the babies. Honestly, sometimes I wonder if she's beginning to go senile already.

Anyway, ever since then she's been very loathe to go to the vet's, and tonight was no exception. She was determined that there was a simple explanation for Rover's peculiar behaviour.

It was very hard to get him to do anything at all. All he wanted to do was lie down. He trailed around after us, walking to heel and practising his 'Comes' but all with his tail between his legs and the most woebegone expression.

'Wow, Kate,' said BDM excitedly. 'I think we're really getting somewhere. He's really settling down.'

'I think he's ill, Mum,' I said.

'But his nose is wet and he doesn't feel hot. There can't be anything seriously wrong.'

'I think there is, Mum. I think we should take him home.'

'Kate, if you want to go home, just go – but don't make out it's because the dog's ill, all right? He's just a bit tired and he's learning how he's meant to behave.'

I wanted a second opinion. Greg was standing close by,

supposedly ready to hand out some toys but really trying to catch Carly's eye at every opportunity.

'Greg,' I hissed. 'Come here a minute, will you?'

He ambled over. He didn't look pleased.

'Greg, I think there's something wrong with Rover,' I said anxiously. 'What do you think?'

He shrugged. 'Seems all right to me,' he said, looking past Rover and smiling at Carly who I could sense was watching us closely. 'Just a bit quiet. Maybe he's tired.'

'There, Kate,' said BDM. 'Now stop fussing. He'll be fine.'

'But you haven't looked at him properly,' I said in frustration to Greg's back. He had wandered over to Carly and was making a big fuss of letting her precious pooch choose its toy.

'I'm going to ask his mum,' I said fiercely to BDM but just then, Mrs Barker started explaining the next exercise and the moment was lost.

I was furious. Greg, who is supposed to be a dog-lover, had done no more than glance at Rover, he was so busy mooning over Carly, and Mum was determined to pretend there wasn't a problem at all.

'I'm taking him home!' I snarled at Mum and started to lead Rover towards the door. Obviously desperate to go, Rover put on a slight turn of speed.

'What on earth are you doing?' demanded BDM. 'I'll say if we're going home, if you don't mind! There's nothing at all the matter with him. Look at him – he's got a real spring in his step!'

'Only because he knows I'm taking him home!'

Rover whined and pulled on his lead.

'Look, he wants to go,' I pleaded.

'Don't be ridiculous, Kate. He's whining because you're pulling him away and he wants to stay!'

By now, of course, people had stopped what they were doing and were listening to us arguing.

'If you don't mind,' said Greg's mum testily, 'we're in the middle of a class.'

'I do apologize,' said BDM. 'Kate, just go home on your own for now, we'll talk about this later.'

Sometimes I make a hole and then I just keep digging. I mean, what's wrong with me? Greg was watching, Cute Carly was watching, Lousy Lisa was watching – and a few weeks ago I wouldn't have cared whether Rover lived or died.

'No,' I said loudly. 'Rover needs to go home. He's coming with me.'

'Kate, please go home. Don't you think I've had enough stress recently?' BDM's voice was chilly enough to freeze a geyser. 'Rover will be fine here with me.'

I won't repeat what I said next. Suffice to say, it was very rude. I completely lost it. The rotten day with Vicky, the fact that Greg was with Carly, the lecture I'd had about LOVE, the niggling worry about Chas, the pitiful expression in

Rover's eyes and now Mum dressing me down in public when she was so clearly wrong – it was too much.

'Love?' I screamed at her. 'Love is patient, love is kind… you don't even know how to love a *dog*, let alone a human! I'm going home and if Rover dies, it'll be *all your fault*!

There was only one way to go after that. Out of the training barn – fast!

I ran all the way home, too furious for tears, but when I got to our front gate and collapsed against it, that's when I began to cry. I suddenly remembered the last time I'd come home from dog-training without Mum – I'd been with Greg. How could things have changed so much so fast?

It was Dad who sorted things out.

'Uh oh,' he said, intercepting me on the landing as I blundered to my room. 'Is it the dog or is it the mother?'

'Both,' I exploded and burst into a fresh storm of sobs. Hayley, who Dad had snuggled in a big towel against his chest, promptly joined in.

Dad groaned. 'Come on,' he said. 'You'd better tell me all about it while I sort Hayley out.'

I followed him into his bedroom, where Ben was wrestling Comet into a clean baby-gro.

'Reveal all, then,' he said, grinning at me. 'Which one bit you?'

Dad scowled at him. 'Take your little sister away and do something wonderful with her,' he said. 'Kate needs to talk.'

'Anything for a quiet life,' said Ben, scooping up Comet. 'Come on, Comet. Nasty doggy and nasty Mummy upset poor little Katie-watie. Or maybe it was nasty Greggy-weggy…'

'Benjamin,' said Dad dangerously. 'Shut up!'

'Sorry,' said Ben, ostentatiously tip-toeing out, but I could still hear him as he walked along the landing going, 'Grr. Kill nasty Greggy-weggy – grr, kill. Rabies, foam, foam, grr, kill…' I suppose it's his idea of expressing sympathy.

'So,' said Dad, plonking Hayley down on the bed and reaching for a nappy. 'Tell me all about it then.'

By the time, Rover and Mum got home, I was in the bath with a large mug of hot chocolate. I could vaguely hear Dad talking to Mum as she settled down to feed the babies – lots of indignant Mum punctuated by soothing Dad noises. I decided there and then that I was going to have an early night and be sound asleep if she came to check up on me. Today had gone on long enough.

That plan worked better than I expected. If Mum did come to speak to me, I never knew. I fell asleep almost as soon as I hit the bed and didn't wake until the early hours of the morning. I'm used to waking up in the small hours. Usually it's one of the babies that disturbs me and I just roll over and go back to sleep. This time was different. I wasn't sure what had woken me – it was a sound that I couldn't quite place. I listened hard. Nothing. I was just about to snuggle down again when I remembered Rover. Perhaps it was him.

I grabbed my bathrobe and staggered out onto the landing, listening all the time. Rover must have heard me for he suddenly gave the most pathetic little whimper. I hurried down the stairs and switched on the hall light.

Urgh! Horrible! Poor old Rover was trapped in his crate with a revolting pool of vomit. I must have heard him retching – and was heartily wishing I hadn't. Well, there was nothing else for it. I would just have to sort him out. Mum and Dad have enough broken nights without mopping up dog sick. I may be a moody teenager but I'm not completely heartless.

I was just wondering how best to tackle it when I heard Mum and Dad's door open. Then Dad stuck his head over the banister.

'Kate? What's up?'

'It's Rover. He's been sick. I *said* he was ill.'

'Hang on. I'm coming down.'

With Dad to help it was far easier to clean up. On my own, I hadn't dared open the crate in case Rover bolted out, straight through all the mess. Before very long, we'd made a clean bed, and Rover slunk back into it and buried his face in his paws.

'D'you think we should call the vet?' I asked.

Dad shook his head. 'I don't think so – not at this time of night. He's probably just eaten some rubbish. He's half-Labrador. They'll eat anything. With luck, he'll be better by the morning now he's been sick. Come on, time you were back in bed.'

He sighed and pushed me in the direction of the stairs. I stomped up them miserably. I could feel Dad's weariness in his push. I knew he was regretting adopting Rover.

But me? How did I feel now? I tossed and turned but I couldn't get back to sleep. I kept seeing Rover's miserable eyes, as he glanced up at me before settling down on his clean bed with a great shudder. I was desperately worried about him but that wasn't the only problem. He had reminded me all too clearly of someone else I was fond of – someone who until not very long ago, had been probably the most important person in my life – Chas.

9

My Mum and I Fight - Again!

Rover didn't seem any better in the morning. For the first time ever, he didn't want to be let out of his crate and showed no interest in his breakfast. Frisk paced past him in a most superior way and I'll swear her lip curled. Rover didn't bat an eyelid.

Dad rang the vet while Mum glowered at him.

'He says give it forty-eight hours,' he reported. 'If he's no better then, we've got to take him in.'

'That's just what I thought,' said BDM. 'Honestly, what a fuss! If one of the kids was sick in the night, we wouldn't be ringing the doctor in the morning! It's just some bug or something he's eaten.'

I guess she's right. He'll probably be fine in a couple of days, but there's something terribly oppressive about having a dog that just lies around looking at you pitifully. At least a human will hide in their room or while away the time with a pile of videos when they're ill! And it felt so quiet without Rover bumbling around with his happy-doggy grin, despite having two rowdy babies in the house. Even they seemed subdued. Until he was poorly, I hadn't noticed how much they like him. Just watching him wag his great hairy tail is an entertainment for them.

I wondered about pretending to be ill myself. Can humans pick up bugs from dogs? The Vicky-Carly-Greg situation at school wasn't exactly appealing and I was genuinely worried about Rover.

Nic saw me crouching by Rover's crate.

'He will be all right, Kate,' he said. 'Don't worry. Dogs are very strong.'

'I didn't think I cared about him,' I said. 'I mean, I never used to like dogs.'

Nic shrugged. 'Love is full of surprises,' he said.

I pretended to gag. Puke! Not someone else telling me about love.

'Go to school, Kate. You'll be late. If he gets worse, I will take him to the vet myself.'

'You will?'

'Of course. Now go.'

And I had to leave it at that. All I could do was pray.

Walking into school, I saw Greg just ahead of me – alone. It was too good an opportunity to miss, despite the fact that I was cringing with embarrassment over last's night scene.

'Greg!' I called.

He turned. 'Hi Kate,' he said, all smiles. Either he was being very tactful or I featured so low on his list of significant people that he'd already forgotten my public fight with Mum.

'Greg, I want to ask you about Rover,' I said.

Greg looked as if he was yawning with his mouth shut. 'Kate, you don't think you're getting just a bit obsessed with that dog, do you?' he said.

The cheek of it! When he has two massive hounds of his own! Granted, he doesn't talk about them much in school, but still!

'Of course not!' I snapped, blushing angrily. 'I'm just concerned because he's been sick. I want to know what you think.'

'Go on then – but I'm not a vet, you know.'

'That's just it. The vet says to leave him for forty-eight hours – it's probably just something he's eaten – but I think it's more serious than that.'

Greg looked irritated. He was probably anxious to find Carly before registration.

'If that's what the vet says, then do it! Sounds very sensible to me.'

He was increasing his pace as he spoke and, without grabbing hold of his arm, I had no choice but to leave it at that. I couldn't help noticing how different he seemed from the sympathetic boy who'd walked me home the night Gran had been taken ill. I know Rover's only a dog, but you'd have thought Greg might be more concerned about a dog he knew than a Granny he didn't. Unless he was trying to impress me that night and now he didn't need to any more. With a sudden pang, I realized how very lonely I was feeling.

The day dragged by. Vicky still seemed to be sulking so at lunchtime I took myself off to the library to do some homework. After ten minutes of failing to learn any new French vocabulary, I took a sheet of paper out of my science file.

'Dear Chas', I wrote and then ground to a halt. It was just like trying to talk to him – I didn't know what to say any more. I wanted to tell him about Rover but he'd made it very clear he didn't like the poor old pooch. I wanted to tell him how sore I felt about Greg and Cute Carly but maybe that wasn't very tactful. I wanted to know if Vicky was right and he really was missing me or if – as I suspected – he'd met all these sophisticated pony club types and had outgrown us all back home. But how could I ask him that?

I chewed my pen for ages and got through several pieces of paper making false starts. Then I threw them all in the bin and decided to phone home.

I was lucky. Nic answered.

'How's Rover?' I demanded.

'Not good. He was sick again.'

'Will you take him to the vet?'

'He is not worse, Kate. He's just not better. Give him a bit more time.'

'I've given him a bit more time!'

'Forty-eight hours?'

'You said, if he was worse…'

'He is not worse. Stop worrying, Kate. He will be all right.'

My money ran out. I do wish Mum and Dad would let me have a mobile. There was nothing I could do and lessons didn't start again for another ten minutes. There's probably nowhere more depressing than a school on a winter's day, when you've fallen out with your friend, when the boy you fancy has gone off with someone else and you think your dog is dying. Or if there is, I don't want to know about it. It was a huge relief to go to afternoon lessons. I must be a very sad case.

Actually, given the same friend-boy-dog scenario, your own cosy bedroom isn't much better. That's where I am now, trying to take my mind off my woes. Rover is fast asleep in his crate ('It must be a bug – he's sleeping it off,' says BDM) but I'm still worried about him. And I've tried to write to Chas again – hopeless. I want to ring Vicky but she was so frosty with me today, I wouldn't dare. The way I feel at the moment, if I was offered a fortnight's luxury holiday on the

Costa Packet, it might as well be a one-way ticket to the local sewage farm.

OK, OK – give me the ticket to the sewage farm, *please!* At least, yesterday was relatively calm and peaceful. This evening has been bedlam *and* I feel like slitting my wrists!

Wednesday evenings are not great at the best of times. Dad has his student night at the salon, Ben has Scouts, Nic has English – and I get to walk Rover – or not, in this case. Rover, though he has stopped throwing up, still refuses to leave his crate. He won't eat and I think he's visibly thinner – so we spent suppertime wrangling about whether he should go to the vet.

'I asked Suzie. She said he should,' said Ben.

'Suzie is not a vet,' said BDM.

'Her dad is.'

'I know that. It was one of his colleagues who was so rude to me the last time I went.'

'I don't think you could say he was rude, dear,' said Dad. 'He was just trying to be helpful.'

'You weren't there,' said BDM. 'He was rude.'

'But you can't let Rover die, just because the vet was rude!' I protested.

'Don't be childish, Kate. I've no intention of letting him die. I just don't want to pay a whacking great vet's bill if it's unnecessary. And it would be very difficult to get him down to the vet's this evening anyway.'

'Can you call one out?' asked Nic.

'At a price,' said Dad.

'I'll help you take him down there, Mum,' I said.

'But the babies need to go to bed. I'm sure it can wait till the morning.'

I looked round the table. I was sure no one else agreed.

'No, it can't,' I said belligerently.

'Don't start, Kate,' said BDM, a warning note in her voice.

But it was too late. I was already on the warpath.

'You know the trouble with this family,' I said, stabbing a chip viciously with my fork. 'You're all wimps! I bet everyone here except Mum thinks Rover should go to the vet right now, but you're all too scared to say anything! Why? Why d'you let her get away with it?'

'This isn't helping, Kate...' interrupted Dad but I ignored him.

'That dog was *her* idea, he's *her* responsibility and she can't even be bothered to take him to the vet when he needs to...'

'Kate, you've said enough. I've told you I'm worried about the expense and I've told you I'm worried about the girls...'

The trouble with Mum and me is we're too alike. I hate admitting it but it's true. Dad says we're like pit bull terriers; we get hold of something and we won't let go. We wind each other up in no time at all. Dad says it's detonate to explosion in less than ten seconds. Tonight was no exception.

'That's just an excuse!' I retorted, standing up and banging my knife on the table. 'You've taken on something you can't handle and you don't want to admit it! But it's poor old Rover who has to suffer!'

Mum was standing by this time too, her whole body quivering with rage – not a pretty sight. Both Hayley and Comet had begun to cry but I could still hear her.

'I have had enough of this,' she stormed. 'You shamed me the other night at the training class and now I can't even have my supper in peace. There is nothing wrong with that dog that can't wait till the morning and it's nothing to do with me not being able to cope. Cope? Cope? It's you that can't cope. You've got in a mess with your friends and you're taking it out on me!'

There was a sudden roar from Dad. 'THAT IS ENOUGH!'

Dad so rarely raises his voice that we were all shocked into silence for a split second. Even the babies were quiet!

'Nic! Ben!' Dad gestured at the twins and without a word the boys started unstrapping them from their high chairs. I collapsed in my seat and hid my head in my hands. I have never seen Dad so angry. His face had gone like Ben's when he's upset – drained of all colour. He waited until the boys had taken Hayley and Comet out and there was silence. Then he spoke, very quietly, but in a voice which made me lose all desire to argue.

'If this…' (he paused to look at Mum and me) '… is what it leads to, then Rover must go back to the dogs' home. I'll give you all one week and then *I* will decide. If I hadn't agreed to us adopting him, he could never have come in the first place. In the meantime, he will go to the vet in the morning – unless he gets significantly worse tonight. And that's final. Now I'm going to the salon.'

With that he stalked out of the kitchen and left Mum and me not knowing quite what to do with ourselves.

There was a hesitant tap on the kitchen door. It was Ben. He had Frisk cuddled against his chest and he was stroking her nervously.

'Er… Nic and I need to go out now,' he said. 'We've put the girls in their bouncing cradles in the lounge, all right?'

'Fine,' said Mum, in a strange, high voice. 'Thanks very much. I'll come straight away. Kate, could you…?'

'I'll clear up in here,' I said hastily. Anything to get away from her.

I had barely cleared the table when the doorbell rang. It used to happen all the time when Mum was working but it's unusual now that she's on maternity leave. Irritated, I dropped the dishcloth I was holding and hurried to open it.

When I saw who it was, I nearly fainted. Leaning against the porch, looking distinctly faint herself, stood Gran.

'Hello dear,' she said, rather breathlessly. 'I thought I'd pop round for a cuppa.'

'You'd better come in,' I said dazedly. I felt as if I was

taking part in some surreal soap opera. Gran had recently been seriously ill, Gran was supposed to be tucked up safely in her cosy nursing home, so what on earth was she doing on our doorstep?

I led her into the lounge and sat her down. Now that she was in the light, I could see that her stockings were splattered with mud and her shoes were soaking.

'How did you get here?' I said, trying to sound as if everything was completely normal.

'Why, I walked of course. It seemed such a pleasant evening.'

Pleasant? It was cold, wet and completely uninviting.

'Yes, of course,' I said. 'Would you like to take your shoes off while I make a cup of tea?'

'That would be very nice, dear. I won't stay long, then I'd better be on my way.'

I hurried into the hall, locked the front door and hid the key. Then I bounded up the stairs two at a time and explained the situation to Mum, who was bathing Hayley while Comet squirmed on the bath mat.

'That's all we need,' said Mum. 'Look, I can't come down just now. Ring the nursing home and, for heaven's sake, don't let her escape!'

When I got downstairs I found Gran bumbling round the kitchen. The phone call would have to wait.

'Let me help you,' I said, casually retrieving the electric kettle from the sink.

Gran had an apron over her coat and was about to turn on the hot tap.

'Dear me, what a mess!' she said. 'You'd better help me clear it away before the men get back from the fields.'

'Of course,' I said and started loading the dishwasher.

She whacked my arm with the dish-mop. 'Not in the cupboard, you silly girl. Bring them to the sink!'

I was just resigning myself to doing the washing up the old way, when Mum burst in, her arms full of babies. She took in the coat, the apron and the hat which Gran still had perched jauntily on her head and raised her eyebrows in despair.

'Mother!' she said cheerily. 'What a pleasant surprise! Would you like to play with the babies while we clear up?'

'Babies?' said Gran. 'What babies? I'm far too busy for babies. There's a war on, you know.'

Mum's eyes met mine.

'I'll go and phone,' I muttered.

The matron at the nursing home was hugely relieved to hear from me. They'd just finished searching the grounds and had been about to call the police.

'I'll send a car round immediately,' she said. 'Can I speak to your mother when Mrs Lofthouse is safely back with us?'

'I'm sure that'll be fine,' I said soothingly. I was so glad not to be the one on the receiving end of BDM's wrath that I could afford to be generous.

Ten minutes later, the car arrived, driven by a very

121

apologetic care assistant. By that time, Gran was busy making huge cheese sandwiches for the men who would be hungry after the haymaking.

'Lovely,' said BDM, ushering Gran into the hall. 'I'm sure they'll enjoy those. Now, here's the car. They'll all be missing you back at the farm.'

'Farm? What farm? Are you feeling all right, Jo, dear? I live in a nursing home now, you know.'

It was one of those increasingly rare lucid moments. The mist had cleared and Gran was back in the here and now. She looked down at Rover in his crate.

'Good God, Jo,' she said. 'What on earth have you been doing to that poor dog? He looks half-starved.'

'Er… he's had a bit of tummy bug actually. Off his food, you know.'

'Off his food? Are you off your head? He'll be off to meet his maker if you don't do something quickly. Look at his eyes.'

We did as we were told. They had an odd, glazed look about them.

'It's no good, Jo,' sighed Gran. 'You'll have to admit it one day. It's a miracle you've managed to keep the children alive, let alone a dog. Thank you for the tea. I'll be off now. My car's waiting.'

Mum closed the door after her and leaned her back against it. The babies, abandoned in the kitchen, began to wail.

Mum looked at Rover and looked at me. She ran her fingers through her spiky hair distractedly. 'Phone the vet, Kate,' she said. 'I'll square it with your dad later.' Then she burst into tears.

10

My Mum and the Runaway

Phew! God moves in a mysterious way, as it says in some old hymn or other. If Gran hadn't turned up when she did, Rover might have been dead by now! Remember he chewed up one of my new trainers? Well, what we didn't realize was that he'd also managed to swallow their plastic bag virtually whole and it was causing a blockage in his gut.

It was Suzie's dad who came out to see him. He was very sympathetic, assured us that there was no way we could have known it was serious (ha! *I* knew all along but at least he made Mum feel better) and then whisked Rover off for an emergency operation to see if his diagnosis was right. I made gallons of tea for Mum while she sat on the sofa, feeding the babies off to sleep and snivelling away about the dreadful evening and that lovely vet. By the time the others got back she was even talking about the wise advice the previous vet had given her! Two-faced or what?

Anyway, I couldn't believe how pleased I was to see Rover when Dad brought him home the next day. He was a bit droopy from the anaesthetic but was clearly delighted to see us, his tail thumping away for the first time in days. Once he was wide awake again, the vet's instructions to keep him quiet were a joke. He was clearly bent on making up for lost time and careered round the house making the twins shriek with delight and the rest of us cringe at the thought of what he might do to his stitches. Frisk was not impressed. She'd clearly thought he had gone for good and was disgusted to see him back. To her evident satisfaction, he tired easily and it wasn't long before he crept into his crate. But this time I wasn't worried. In fact, I was so thrilled with his recovery that the next day, I couldn't resist describing the drama to Greg in registration.

He shrugged. 'Well, what d'you expect with a dog that's half-Labrador? They're like goats – they eat anything. Give me a Newfoundland any day.'

I fired up in Rover's defence. Suddenly, Chloe and Biggles didn't seem quite as delightful as I'd thought. 'Well, at least he doesn't slaver all over the place,' I said. And then, remembering Carly's precious poodle… 'And at least he's got a sensible haircut.'

'There is nothing wrong with Chloe and Biggles' coats,' snapped Greg. 'They're meant to be shaggy.'

'Didn't say they weren't,' I said, bored with the

conversation. I drifted away. Suddenly, I couldn't see why I'd been so attracted to Greg. OK, so he was handsome and, superficially, he'd been very charming – but it was very much a charm he could turn on and off at will. He didn't seem like the sort of person who'd stand by you through thick and thin. Thinking that sent an arrow of guilt shooting painfully through me. Maybe I wasn't that sort of person either. I'd always meant to be – but now? The words of Mum's card flashed through my mind. The card might be tacky but the words... some of them... I just couldn't forget. 'Love is patient, love is kind... it always protects, always trusts, always hopes, always perseveres. Love never fails.' I'd been there for Rover but what about Vicky? And Chas? I made up my mind. I would find Vicky the moment registration was over – so what if I was late for my first lesson? 'Love always perseveres.' And Chas? That was more difficult. What *was* going on with him? But tonight I would write to him. Definitely. Even if it took all night. 'Love is not easily angered, it keeps no score of wrongs... it always hopes.'

That's what I intended anyway. But as Gran says, 'The road to hell is paved with good intentions.' Took me years to work out what she was going on about. Cheery little thought, isn't it? Not.

Anyway, I couldn't find Vicky anywhere. I thought maybe she was avoiding me and didn't give up until well after the bell had gone. 'Love always perseveres.' When I finally went to my lesson (and got thoroughly told off in front of Lousy Lisa – 'Love is not proud' I kept telling myself bitterly, through clenched teeth), I realized what should have been obvious. Vicky wasn't even in school. Normally, we ring each other if we're ill but things aren't normal any more. I nearly rang her at lunchtime but lost my nerve at the last minute and decided to leave it until the evening. The fact that she was off school was a good excuse to pop round to see her. But even that plan didn't work.

I'd decided I would have my tea and then go. I needed to psych myself up. In the meantime, I would start a letter to Chas. The sooner I did that, the better. I decided to tell him all about the drama with Rover – and all about Cute Carly and Greg. That's what I would have done before he went away. I'd have told him everything. I couldn't handle the new Chas, so I would write to the old one and see what happened. Once I'd decided that, the words seemed to pour out of me. I found myself telling him all about how confused I'd felt in the last few weeks – about Greg, about Rover, about him – even about love. It was a wrench to go down and eat and I decided I would have to finish my letter before I went out to see Vicky. I was on the final paragraph when I heard the doorbell. It was that time of night again – the time that Gran had turned up. Mum and Nic were bathing the babies, Dad was out with Rover and Ben had gone to see Suzie.

'Dear God, please don't let it be Gran again,' I prayed as

I ran down the stairs to answer it. 'Please let her be all right.'

It was a horrid night, freezing cold and with a bitter wind which took my breath away as I opened the door. Perhaps it would be Dad back early with Rover.

It wasn't. The person on the doorstep had his jacket pulled up round his ears but I knew who he was.

'Chas!' I said. 'What on earth are *you* doing here?'

Chas made a bitter sound somewhere between a harsh laugh and a sob. 'I've run away,' he said, barely audibly. 'I'm not going back.'

I could tell that he was really struggling not to cry. I was horrified.

'You'd better come in,' I said. 'I'll get Mum.'

'No, I wanted to…'

'Who is it?' called BDM, leaning over the banister.

Chas almost gave up the struggle. Tears ran down his cheeks but he brushed them away furiously. 'It's me,' he said, looking up at her. 'I'm sorry to be a nuisance, Mrs Lofthouse.'

Mum was already bounding down the stairs. 'Kate, go and help Nic,' she said briskly. Then she put an arm round Chas's shoulders and propelled him into the kitchen. 'Come on,' she said. 'You'd better tell me what's been going on.'

I ran up the stairs. 'Please Nic,' I begged. 'Can you manage on your own?'

'Probably. Why?'

'Chas is downstairs. He's run away from school.'

Nic raised his eyebrows.

'Mum's swept him off to the kitchen. She's probably doing the Spanish Inquisition – but I think he wanted to talk to *me*.'

Nic nodded. 'Go down then. I'll be fine.'

I know you're not supposed to eavesdrop but on this occasion I tried. I was sure Chas had been about to say he wanted to talk to me, before Mum started interfering. And what was she going to say? You know what grown-ups are like. You've started so you must finish. Finish the year or the term or the course or whatever it is they've paid for. It doesn't matter if their money is paying for your nervous breakdown. And in Chas's case, there was all that wretched uniform to think of too! If it was me, I'd make a generous gift of it to some freezing orphans somewhere, rather than use it as a weapon for torturing Chas – but grown-ups never see things in quite the same way. I could just imagine all the things Mum might be saying. She'd be talking about perseverance, character-building, determination, courage and six years being only a short time if you thought in terms of eternity. Well OK, but when you're only thirteen, six years feels like the rest of your life!

Unfortunately, our kitchen door is pretty solid and I couldn't hear enough to make sense but I knew from the tone of Mum's voice that Chas was getting the old pull-yourself-together treatment. There'd be tea and chocolate biscuits but that's where the sympathy would stop.

Just as I was beginning to think I'd explode with anger and frustration and burst into the kitchen whether Mum liked it or not, Dad got back with Rover.

'Hello,' said Dad curiously, as I guiltily stooped to give Rover a rather over-enthusiastic welcome. 'What's going on here?'

I explained quickly and was just adding, 'But I think he really wanted to talk to me…', when the phone rang. Dad got there first.

'Well, yes he is. As a matter of fact, he's talking to Jo… oh, so he's come here straight from school… right… yes, well, I'm sure that should be possible. Sorry – I was out when he came, I'll have a word with Jo… no, no trouble at all. I'll ring you when I've spoken to them then. All right? … yes, goodbye.'

He put the receiver down. 'Chas's mum,' he said.

'Obviously. What's all this about you speaking to Mum?'

'She wants us to take him home.'

'I don't think he'll want to do that. Not if he didn't go there in the first place.'

'I know, but he is her son. We can't refuse to take him back.'

'Maybe she'd agree to him staying here for the night while he calms down or something?'

'Maybe. I'd better speak to Jo.'

We'd been too busy talking to notice what was happening behind the kitchen door. Suddenly it was wrenched open and Chas burst out.

'Was that my mother on the phone?' he demanded. 'Or the school?'

'It was your mother,' said Dad. 'Now just take things easy, Chas. Just calm down a bit, OK?'

But Chas was beside himself. 'Did you tell her I was here? Did you?'

'Well, yes I did. She was very worried, you know, Chas…'

Chas swore horribly. 'I came here because I wanted to talk to Kate and I thought you'd help,' he shouted, 'but instead I've had a lecture and now you've shopped me! I thought you were my friends!'

And before any of us could stop him, he tore open the front door and rushed out into the freezing darkness.

Mum stood in the doorway of the kitchen, her face flushed. 'Go after him, for goodness' sake!' she exclaimed. 'I can't – I have to feed the babies!'

But Dad hesitated. 'I don't think he wants that, Jo. I think he needs some space. He's a big lad and it's not late. When he's calmed down, he'll either come back here or go home. What else can he do? He can't stay out long – it's freezing.'

Mum snorted. 'Well, *you* can ring up and explain that to his parents!' she said. 'How would you feel if it was Ben?'

'I'm thinking how I'd feel if it was me,' he said. 'I've run away from school and the people I was relying on to help me have just let me down big-time – or that's how I see it. I've cried in front of them, I've sworn at them and I feel like an all-round failure. I think I'd just want a bit of space to consider my next move.'

Mum and I looked at each other. I could see the sense of what Dad was saying. So could she, I could tell. If it was me, I'd want someone to run after me, find me, love me better and sort it all out. But Chas isn't like that. He's a boy who has his own den to hide in when things get too much. Maybe he was going there now.

'It's just that it's so cold and wet,' said Mum. 'And he was in such a state.'

Dad shrugged. 'Well, it's too late now. We don't know where he's gone. If we end up calling the police, then so be it. But my guess is, we won't have to. He's a level-headed boy on the whole and he knows he's got to find a solution. He's not going to hitch a lift to find his fortune in London or anything silly like that. I think he'll go home. He'll be fine.'

Mum nodded. So did I. It all sounded so sensible. And I trust Dad. But for once he was wrong.

I didn't want to go back to my room. I couldn't face that almost finished letter. Instead, I whistled to Rover and went into the lounge to watch TV. Rover isn't allowed on the furniture so I lay on the floor with him and tried to take my mind off Chas. I could hear Dad having a lengthy telephone conversation with Mrs Peterson and wondered if we'd all be donning wellies and waterproofs to form a search party before long. Instead, when he finally put the phone down, I heard him go quietly into the kitchen. From upstairs came the faint strains of Nic practising his cello. Peace was beginning to settle on the house – except in the lounge.

I simply couldn't get Chas out of my mind. I agreed with everything Dad said. Chas is (or was) a great friend partly because he's so level-headed. In the same position, I might be going for the dramatic gesture – threatening to throw myself off a bridge or something – but not Chas. He'd mooch around and finally take himself off to his den. In the morning, he might be prepared to talk. That was the likely sequence of events. But my imagination ran riot. He might be abducted, he might completely flip and throw himself under a train, he might walk blindly into oncoming traffic – there was no limit to the sticky ends I could foresee. As if that wasn't enough, Rover wouldn't settle either. I'd thought that he might like a nice soothing cuddle but he kept pacing round the room and whimpering at the door.

'D'you want to go in your crate?' I asked at last, letting him into the hall. No, it wasn't that. He sat down by the front door and looked up at me hopefully. Did he want to go out? He was on a special recovery diet and Suzie's dad had politely explained that he might need to 'toilet' more often.

I got down Rover's lead and he positively grinned. Well,

a walk would suit me. We might even run into Chas.

'Dad,' I said, sticking my head round the kitchen door. 'I'm just taking Rover out for a bit.'

Dad had the radio on and was busy with a pile of ironing. He nodded. 'Don't be too long,' he said.

I opened the door to an icy blast. The bitter wind had sharpened and it was raining in that splodgy way which makes you wish it would snow properly and get it over with. I shuddered and hoped Rover would soon do what he had to do or walk off his restlessness. With a bit of luck, by the time we got back, Mrs Peterson would have rung to say Chas was safely home.

Rover bounded out but then stopped to sniff excitedly at something halfway up the path.

'Come on, Rover,' I said impatiently. 'It's freezing out here.'

But Rover made no move.

I tugged at his lead. 'What is it anyway?' I said.

I stooped to look. It was a glove. Chas's probably. He must have dropped it as he rushed out. I shivered. I didn't like the thought of Chas out for long in this, especially with only one glove.

I put it in my pocket and was almost pulled off my feet as Rover made a sudden bolt for the gate.

'Hey, slow down, boy!' I shouted as he dragged me out into the street. 'What's happened to all our training?'

But no amount of telling would persuade him to slow

down. He was really pulling on his lead and I wondered if his traumatic experience had made him forget everything we'd taught him. I tried stopping every time he pulled but it was incredibly frustrating and we were getting nowhere. In the end, I let him have his way and trotted along behind him. We could sort out his bad habits when it wasn't so cold and wet.

We were heading for the park but I had no intention of going in on such a dark and miserable night. I expected a battle when we got there and was very surprised when Rover peeled off to the right at the gates. That didn't suit me either. I was ready to go home and see if the phone had rung.

'Come on, Rover, home-time!' I said brightly, hauling on his lead. 'Come on now, home!'

But Rover refused to come. He whined and whimpered and pulled, still determined to go right. In the end, he plonked himself down on his bottom and refused to move, except to paw persistently at my leg.

'Rover, for goodness' sake, what is it?' I demanded. 'I want to go home and see if there's been a call about Chas!'

And that was when the penny finally dropped. It'd taken long enough! If you turn right at the park, the road leads into open country. The pavement runs out; that's why I didn't want to go that way on such a bad night. It's also the road that leads to the Petersons' farm.

'Chas!' I whispered. 'Rover, has something happened to Chas?'

Rover whined and pawed at my leg some more.

I pulled out Chas's glove for him to sniff and the next moment, we were running, Rover leading the way as fast as he could with stitches in his tummy.

'Dear God, let Chas be all right!' I said, over and over in my head, alternating with 'And, dear God, please let Rover be all right too!'

'Chas!' I shouted out loud, once we were away from the houses. 'Chas! Where are you?' We were having to go more carefully now. The edges of the road were boggy with autumn's dead leaves. I wished I'd thought of bringing a torch but I hadn't been intending to leave the street lights behind. Please God, I was thinking, don't let it be much further. I was convinced now that I was going to find Chas dismembered at the very least. There could be no other explanation for Rover's bizarre behaviour.

'Chas!' I shouted desperately, forced to stop for a moment to wipe wet hair from my eyes and to catch my breath. 'Chas! Where are you?'

A car swept by, blinding me with its headlights and making me jump to the side. A great slurry of filthy water splattered my legs and Rover – and his wound was supposed to be kept clean! But I couldn't worry about that now and he was frantically urging me on.

'Chas?' I called again, willing him to be nearby. 'Chas! Chas! Where are you?'

And then I heard it, very faintly, but obviously not far away. A weak voice but one I recognized. Just a couple of words, almost lost on the wind.

'Down here!' Chas called. And again. 'Down here!'

11

The Runaway and Me

Down here! Chas's words echoed horribly in my brain. I didn't want to believe what they must mean. The road lay ahead of us, rising slowly into the hills. They're not big hills but high enough for there to be a steepish drop alongside us.

Rover and I sprang forward. The next moment, Rover was scrabbling frantically at the side of the road, nearly taking me with him. I wrapped an arm round a small tree, clung desperately to his lead and peered into the gloom. Rover was barking furiously; he clearly thought that if I would just let him go, he could stage a rescue attempt, single-pawed.

'Chas?' I called. 'Chas? Are you down there?' It was hard to see clearly but I could detect movement, probably not much more than a metre below me.

'Yes – but I won't be for much longer. This root I'm hanging on to is beginning to crack – I can hear it going.' As Chas spoke, his voice remarkably calm, he lifted his head and I could pick out his face, pale against the darkness.

I felt sick. It wasn't a huge drop to the stream below – maybe ten metres – but it was certainly far enough to injure yourself badly, at the very least!

'I can't get any grip with my feet. It's so wet, they just slip in the clay.'

I could well imagine. Further down the valley, where the stream runs into the park and the sides are not so high, children make brilliant slides in the soft red soil. I've done it myself – it's great fun – but only by choice on a warm, summer's day and even then kids sometimes get hurt. I could imagine the root he was clinging to – smooth and bone-like, as slippery as wet marble in this weather.

'I can't hold on much longer, Kate.' His voice sounded slightly desperate now.

'I know, I know,' I said, feverishly. 'I'm just thinking what to do.' There was no way I could reach him. I was wearing a long scarf but even if I let it down to him, I couldn't support his weight single-handed. And I couldn't risk getting Rover to help me pull because of his stitches – even if I could get him to understand what I meant.

Rover, who had exchanged barking for whining, was still scrabbling in the dirt, hauling on his lead to try to get closer to Chas. His lead! Of course! With that and my scarf together, something might be possible!

'Hang on, Chas! I've thought of something!' I said and grabbed Rover by his collar. 'Sit, Rover, sit! Yes, I know that's Chas down there but if you want to help him you must sit!'

Rover whimpered but stopped scrabbling and did what he was told. As quickly as I could with my numb fingers, I undid his collar and held him still with my arm round his neck. The realization that Chas must have lost virtually all feeling in his hands by now made me resolute.

'Go home, Rover!' I said firmly. 'Go home quickly! Get help!'

Rover looked up at me, clearly puzzled. 'Go home, Rover!' I said, more urgently, pointing back the way we had come and giving him a shove. 'Home now! Go home!'

Rover took a tentative step away from me and looked back over his shoulder.

'That's a good boy,' I said encouragingly, praying that he would understand. 'Go home! Get Dad!'

The next moment, he had gone, running away into the night, as fast as he had brought me here.

I turned back to Chas.

'Listen, Chas,' I said urgently. 'I've sent Rover to get help. Now, I'm going to fasten my scarf and his lead together. It should be long enough to wrap round this tree and still reach you. Then, if you hang on to the collar, I might be able to pull you up.'

'Worth a try,' said Chas. His voice was cracking with the

strain of hanging on. 'But be quick, Kate. Either this root or my fingers are going to give way.'

Suddenly I seemed to be all fingers and thumbs. Tying the scarf to the lead seemed to take forever. Chas didn't nag but I could hear his breathing getting more and more ragged below me. Every tiny noise had me panicking. Every second brought closer the ghastly moment when I'd hear the root break and Chas plummet down the slope.

'It won't be long now,' I said, gasping with relief as I tested my knot. I wrapped my make-shift rope round the trunk of the small tree, made a loop for my wrist in one end of my scarf and then dangled the end with the collar attached down towards Chas.

I couldn't see properly, but I could hear his intake of breath as he took one hand off the root and stretched for the collar.

'Come on, Chas – stretch!' I urged him. 'Come on – you can do it!'

I wished I could let out just a bit of slack – but there wasn't any. I simply had to keep that loop round the tree or we'd both go slithering down the slope.

Would all his weight hanging on one point finish the root off completely? The seconds crept by like years as I listened to Chas straining in the dark. There was an excruciating silence and then…

'Got it!' I went soggy with relief and was almost yanked round the tree-trunk as he transferred his whole weight to my 'rope'. Pulling back as hard as I could, I wished my scarf was long enough to wrap round my waist. It wasn't though. Chas was dependent on one small tree and my puny arms.

'You OK?' I panted.

'Yeah, are you? I've got my wrists through the collar. Can you pull at all? I might be able to find somewhere higher up that I can grip with my feet.'

I tried, I really did, but it was all I could do just to hang on.

'I'm sorry,' I gasped, almost sobbing with effort and disappointment. 'This isn't much better than the root!'

'No way,' panted Chas. 'You should see the state of the root – and it helps to use my wrists.'

'So what now?'

'We just hang on and pray that Rover gets help soon, I guess. Never mind – I always wondered what it felt like to be on the rack.'

I giggled though it wasn't at all funny. I was so het up, it was either giggle or cry.

We were silent for a while. My arms felt as if they were coming out of their sockets so I dreaded to think what Chas's felt like. I silently prayed for help to come soon because I knew that I couldn't support Chas's weight much longer, even with the tree's help. That grim thought loosened my tongue. It could be now or never to sort things out with Chas.

'Chas,' I said. 'Can you hear me?'

There was a grunt from below.

'Chas, since you went away – what's been wrong? Why have you been so funny with me?'

'Me? Funny with you? You hardly wrote to me!'

'But I did! I did! And when you came home, you hardly spoke to me!'

'You didn't seem interested in me any more.' It was clearly a huge effort for him to speak but he persevered. 'You seemed so busy – with Rover, with that boy Greg. And at the disco I could hardly get near you for boys!'

'But you didn't make any effort to get near me! You seemed perfectly happy with Vicky!'

'I wasn't going to come begging, Kate. Out of sight, out of mind. Maybe I've been cramping your style. I had this letter from Lisa. She said…'

I nearly let go of the rope.

'Chas! You never believed something Lisa wrote! You know she hates my guts!'

'I know, I know, I tried not to.' Chas's voice was lame. 'But when I came home – well, you didn't seem the same. Like you weren't that interested in me any more…'

'Oh, don't be so silly – you know how much I hated the thought of you going away!'

'That wasn't the message I got the night before I went.'

I could feel myself blushing in the dark as I remembered.

'Oh that! Well, I guess I was just embarrassed… I mean, you've never hugged me before…' I tailed off feebly.

'So what's all this about Greg then?' Chas's voice had been strained all along but he was clearly nearing the end of his strength now.

'Oh, I don't know, I...' I was floundering, not knowing how to answer. Half my mind was taken up with a kind of constant nagging prayer that help would get here *now*. How could I explain how I'd felt about Greg? That I'd thought I was in love but now was pretty sure that Ben was right and that love hadn't had much to do with it at all. If I loved any boy apart from Ben, it was the one whose life hung on the end of my scarf right now. What was it? Love always protects, always trusts, always hopes, always perseveres? Something like that anyway. Could I launch into an explanation of all that now? At least the darkness would spare my blushes.

Just then, I heard the sound I'd almost given up waiting for.

'Kate! Kate! Where are you? Are you there?'

It was Dad. The next moment, a very tired Rover flopped down beside me and tried to lick my boots.

Dad, armed with a powerful torch, took in the situation at a glance.

'Hang on, Chas,' he said encouragingly. 'Not much longer now.' Then he helped me unloop my hands and took Chas's weight himself.

'When you're ready, Kate, we'll pull together. He should come up easily enough and then you can give him a hand, while I take the strain.'

I shook my arms and rubbed them as hard as I could. The blood came flooding back to them in an agonizing rush.

'OK,' I said, wincing. 'I'm ready.'

I took hold of my loop again and Dad got a grip further along the scarf. 'One, two, three, pull!' he said and Chas came slithering up the bank towards us. Moments later, I'd let go of my loop and was helping him clamber up onto the side of the road, where he collapsed, his arms still stretched out in front of him, groaning.

'I don't think I'll ever feel my arms again,' he moaned.

Rover, his tiredness forgotten at the sight of a rescued Chas, was trying to lick his face furiously. Chas, temporarily helpless, let him, while Dad gently massaged some life back into his arms.

'Stop it, Rover,' I told him. 'Leave Chas alone. He doesn't even *like* you.'

Chas rolled awkwardly onto his side. 'Kate, I know you've just rescued me and I should be nice to you, but sometimes you are incredibly stupid,' he said. 'I've always liked Rover, actually, and I like him even more after what he's just done.'

How's that for gratitude? And why on earth was I getting called stupid again?

I found out a couple of days later – a couple of days which, despite the pain in my shoulders and arms, were probably two of the happiest of my life. What had happened was easily explained. Just as Dad had thought, Chas had set out to walk home. He reckoned that, as his parents knew he was safe, he would simply sit it out in his den until they saw reason. Unfortunately, a car had swept down the hill, forcing him to leap aside – in a place where leaps were best avoided. The rest is history, except that Dad, suddenly ill at ease, had decided to set out to look for Chas or Rover and me. By that stage he was anxious about all of us. He spotted Rover racing back home but the heroic hound had refused to get in the car. Superdog, or what? Eventually he persuaded Dad to follow him – just in time. Was it all an answer to my prayers? I guess it probably was. The thing is, that when I remember to pray, life seems to get surprisingly full of coincidences.

We all staggered back to the car and returned home to find both BTM and Mrs Charming installed in our kitchen, about to send for the police. Instead they sent for the doctor.

Fortunately, the next day was Saturday but it wasn't until after lunch that Mum agreed to let me see Chas.

'You can't go barging in first thing,' she insisted. 'They have a lot of sorting out to do. I'm sure they'll ring before long – they must know how anxious we are.'

Waiting for the phone to ring was unbearable, so in the end I did what I'd promised myself I'd do the day before – I went round to see Vicky.

As I walked up the path, I had so many butterflies in my

stomach I'm surprised I didn't take off! I kept my eyes rooted firmly to the ground; I really didn't want to catch a glimpse of Vicky peering at me from behind a curtain.

Vicky's mum was as welcoming as ever.

'Why, Kate, how lovely to see you! Vicky will be so pleased. She's feeling much better now.'

'What was the matter with her?' I croaked.

'One of her migraine attacks, I'm afraid. She'd got herself all worked up about something and when she gets like that, it always ends up with her being ill. You don't know what's been wrong, do you?'

I studied the doorstep, blushing furiously. 'I'm afraid we haven't really been speaking since the night of the disco. You remember we had an argument and she came home on her own...?'

'Yes, of course, but I thought that was some problem about a boy?'

'Well, yes, that as well, I think – but I'm afraid I haven't really helped.'

'Oh well, Kate, never mind. These things happen. Come in and sort it out and I'm sure you'll both feel a lot better. Would you like a drink of something?'

I smiled gratefully at Vicky's mum. I'd been feeling so bad about the whole thing, it was a relief to hear someone make it sound normal.

'I'd love a cup of tea, please,' I said. 'Is Vicky in her room?'

'No, I'm not,' said Vicky, suddenly appearing at the top of the stairs.

It was an awkward moment. Vicky's mum tactfully disappeared into the kitchen.

'What are you here for?' asked Vicky stiffly.

I'd been rehearsing what I was going to say, all the way over – all about how I'd wanted to find her yesterday and that I was really sorry and that I would try to be a better friend in the future. Instead, I just blurted out, 'Chas ran away.'

'What?' exclaimed Vicky. She bounded down the stairs two at a time. 'Is he all right?'

'Yes, but he nearly wasn't.'

Vicky grabbed my arm and pulled me through into their lounge. 'Tell me everything,' she insisted. 'Every single gory detail.' So I did.

When I'd finished, she sat back and let out a long, low whistle. 'He was very lucky – you both were. He could have pulled you down there too!'

'I don't think it would have killed us.'

'Maybe not but still… Rover's turning out to be a real pooch to be proud of, isn't he?'

I smiled. 'He certainly is,' I said. 'I was *so* glad we hadn't sent him back to the dogs' home. I'd hate him to go anyway – I really love having him now. But what about Chas? I thought he didn't like Rover? What did I say that was so stupid?'

'Oh, work it out for yourself, Kate. He's quite right, you can be pretty stupid. Like I said after the disco.'

'Don't start that again. I came to say sorry.'

'Go on then.'

'I'm sorry.'

'So am I.'

'You don't need to say sorry. You had a reason to be fed up.'

'Yes, but I didn't have to take it out on you all week.'

'No, but…'

'Oh shut up, Kate. Friends?'

'Of course. I was miserable as hell, this week.'

'I suppose Greg going off with Carly didn't help?'

I shook my head. 'Forget it. I've seen right through him. He just thinks he's God's gift to girls. I bet you anything he'll have finished with Carly in a fortnight and be after someone else. Not me though.'

'And not me either,' agreed Vicky. 'I couldn't have put it better myself.'

We grinned foolishly at each other.

'Better luck next time, eh?' I said.

'You don't *need* better luck,' said Vicky. 'Anyway, hadn't you better go? Chas might have rung by now.'

I glanced at my watch and gasped. 'Too right! Look, I'll ring you as soon as I know what's going on, all right?'

'If you don't, I'll kill you!'

It was so good to be friends again.

12

Chas, Mum and Me

'Well?' I demanded, bursting into our kitchen where lunch was happening in its usual messy, noisy way, though minus Rover who was still sleeping off his exertions in the hall.

'Chas wants you to go over,' chorused Mum, Nic and Ben.

'But does he have to go back to school?'

'He wants you to go over,' they all chorused again.

'I hate you lot,' I said. 'Can't you just tell me?'

'We don't know!' said Ben indignantly. 'He wants to talk to you first! Can't think why. If I'd been there, I'd have clung on to the tree and let him climb up my legs, not kept him dangling on the end of a dog lead for hours.'

'It wasn't hours, clever-clogs, and you weren't there so shut up!'

'You did very well, Kate,' said Mum soothingly. 'Ben's only jealous because he missed all the excitement.'

'Excitement?' echoed Ben. 'I'd rather watch paint dry –

well, actually, I'd rather snog Suzie…'

'Ben!' said Mum warningly but I didn't stay for any more. I'd made myself a sandwich, grabbed an apple and a packet of crisps and was ready to go.

'Don't you want to wait for a lift?' exclaimed Mum. 'You're still looking tired!'

'I'll cycle,' I said.

'Aren't your arms too sore?'

They *were* sore – they felt dreadful actually – but I wanted to go immediately.

Nic stood up. 'I will take you, Kate,' he said. 'Come on, let's go.'

Driving past the scene of last night's drama, I could barely pick out the place where Chas had slipped.

'You were very lucky,' said Nic, as he changed gear for the hill.

'That's what Vicky said but I don't think luck had much to do with it actually.'

'God again, huh?'

I nodded. 'Doesn't seem to matter how much I ignore him, he doesn't go away,' I said.

'You could say the same about Chas,' said Nic.

A few minutes later, Nic pulled into the farmyard. 'I'll see you later, then,' he said. 'If you need a lift, ring.'

'Wouldn't you like to come in for a minute?' I said, suddenly nervous.

Nic shook his head. 'It's *you* he wants to see,' he said, with a grin.

I stuck out my tongue and got out of the car. Chas was strolling across from his den to meet me. Nic made an OK sign at us and roared off.

Chas and I stood looking at each other awkwardly. Mistake. We should have gone while the going was good. The front door flew open and out burst Mrs Charming Peterson to overwhelm me in a lavender-scented hug against her ample, navy cashmere bosom. I was probably closer to severe bone-fracture than Chas had ever been on the end of my 'rope'!

'Kate! Darling!' she gushed. 'How can we ever thank you enough? You and your daring doggie! Chas has been very silly indeed but it's all sorted out now and we understand each other far better but it could have all ended so differently if it hadn't been for you and your presence of mind and...' On and on she went, with me still clamped against her chest, in ever-increasing danger of suffocation. Over her shoulder I could see Chas rolling his eyes at me and trying not to laugh.

'Mother,' he said, at last. 'Can I talk to Kate now, please? I think she came to see me actually.'

Mrs Charming let go of me so suddenly I nearly fell over.

'Oh, of course, darling. I'm sorry but I just *had* to tell Kate how much...'

'I think she's got the message now, Mum.'

'Yes, thank you, Mrs Peterson,' I gasped, glaring at Chas. 'It was the least I could do.'

'Oh, but…'

Chas steered me firmly towards his den.

'Do let me know when you need a lift home, Kate, dear,' Mrs Charming called after us. 'And you must bring your darling doggie to see us soon!'

We fell onto the battered sofa in Chas's den, narrowly avoiding squashing a couple of cats, and howled with laughter.

'I'm sorry,' I spluttered. 'I know she's your mum but… and anyway, you could have shut her up earlier, you rat. She nearly broke half my ribs!'

'Revenge!' said Chas and threw a cushion at me – so I hurled a manky old pillow at him. When we'd finished fighting we collapsed, panting, side by side on the sofa.

'Oh, it's so good to be back,' gasped Chas.

'So are you back? To stay?'

Chas nodded. 'Dad's furious about the wasted money, of course, but I'm not getting the blame for that. They spent more time arguing with each other than having a go at me this morning.'

'That doesn't sound too good,' I said carefully.

'Oh, they'll be all right,' said Chas, with a shrug. 'Mum admitted it was her fault in the end – though I don't think that's entirely fair. Dad's far too keen on the "anything for a quiet life" approach.'

'Just as long as his pigs are happy,' I said.

'That's about it,' agreed Chas, with a sigh.

'So they don't mind about you running away?'

'Well, I wouldn't say they don't mind, but I think they're so glad I'm safe it's kind of got overlooked. And it turns out Mum missed me horribly.' He looked sideways at me. 'You didn't though, did you?'

'I did,' I said gravely. 'I just didn't realize that was the problem, what with the dog and Greg and everything. I just kept thinking it was hormones making me feel so grumpy, or being in love with Greg or something.'

'But you're not in love with Greg?'

I shook my head. Quickly, to cover my embarrassment, I asked him the question that had been bugging me since last night.

'Why did you call me stupid, Chas? When I said you didn't like Rover?'

'Because it wasn't *Rover* I didn't like, you idiot! It was the way you gave him all your attention and left me out. You know what they say about dogs – a man's best friend…'

'Or a woman's…'

'Exactly. Well, I thought *I* was your best friend. And when I came to that disco – well, it was even worse. Especially after that horrible letter I'd had from Lisa.'

So Vicky had been right all along.

'What did Lisa say exactly?' I asked.

'Oh, just what you'd expect really. Totally two-faced.

How she hoped I wasn't worrying about you missing me because you seemed to be fine and had this great new friend called Greg. That sort of stuff.'

I nearly laughed. 'And I thought you must have found loads of better friends at school! Sophisticated girls without crazy mothers!'

'Of course not, idiot! Would I be here now if I had?'

We were silent for a while.

'Chas,' I said, at last. 'I've got to have other friends as well. So have you.'

'I know that. I was stupid – but I was so fed up and confused and…'

'I know. So was I.'

'So how are you feeling now?'

'Like I've got my best friend back.'

Chas smiled. 'Same here. Guess that'll do for now. Want a coffee?'

I thought about it all while he boiled the water and rummaged around for biscuits. The trouble is, I'm sure there are going to be other boys I'm going to fall for like I fell for Greg – and where's that going to leave Chas? Still my best friend? I keep thinking about what Ben said. 'If you're in love, it's like she's your best friend in all the world – *and* you really fancy her.'

Oh well, I suppose I'll just have to wait and see. As Nic said, love is full of surprises.

***

Late that night, when I was lying in bed going over and over all that had happened, BDM came to see me.

'Kate,' she said, plonking herself down on the end of my duvet. 'I owe you an apology.'

I sat up in surprise.

'What on earth for?' I said.

'For adopting Rover,' she said. 'I owe the whole family an apology.'

'But why? We all love Rover. And Dad has said it's OK for him to stay!'

'I know. But we didn't *all* want him at first – especially not you. Sometimes I'm so busy trying to fix things that I can't work out what's really broken. We've been very fortunate. Rover is going to fit into this family fine, but he very nearly didn't and it would have been my fault. I should never have taken him on at the time I did. It's only because I've got such a fantastic, understanding family that we've managed.'

I was completely speechless. 'But…' I stammered. 'But…'

'But nothing. I was wrong.'

'But if we hadn't taken him in, he might still be stuck at the dogs' home and…'

'Oh, come on, Kate! A lovely young dog like Rover? He'd have soon found a new home. You're just going to have to admit it. I made a big mistake.'

'Well, I won't – not about that anyway. But *dancing* at a school disco, now that's a *big* mistake.'

'Oh, you're so dull, Kate. Just because I'm middle-aged doesn't mean I have to behave like I am, does it? But I was wrong about the dog.'

I wrapped my arms round her in a huge hug.

'OK, Big Dumb Mum, I'll admit it – you were wrong – but I'm so glad you were. Just think where Chas might be now, if we hadn't had Rover. And I still love you even if you are the most embarrassing mother that ever lived.'

Mum laughed. 'So you don't think Rover's the Hound from Hell any more, then?'

'No,' I said, hugging her even tighter. 'If you want my opinion, I think he's very probably the Dog from God.'

My Mum and Other Horror Stories

Meg Harper

'Go and write about it,' said Dad. 'Go on. You
want to be a writer – it'll make a good sitcom one
day. You'll feel a lot better when you've got it off
your chest.'

'I want to write horror stories not sitcoms,'
I said.

'The idea of your mum on that bike *is* a horror
story.'

So Kate begins her hilarious account of life with
her well-meaning but eccentric mum.

ISBN 0 7459 4830 8

My Mum and the Gruesome Twosome

Meg Harper

'I can't believe it! At her age – she's gone and
GOT PREGNANT! I haven't told anyone yet. It's
too embarrassing. I might tell Vicky tomorrow
but I don't expect much sympathy from her. My
last hope is Chas – surely I can rely on him to
understand?'

Being a teenager is difficult enough – without
suddenly finding out that your mum is pregnant.

And then there's new girl, Carly. Chas seems
a bit too keen to help her to settle in, and Kate
feels that her whole life is falling apart…

ISBN 0 7459 4829 4

All Lion books are available from your local bookshop, or can be ordered via our website or from Marston Book Services. For a free catalogue, showing the complete list of titles available, please contact:

Customer Services
Marston Book Services
PO Box 269
Abingdon
Oxon
OX14 4YN

Tel: 01235 465500
Fax: 01235 465555

Our website can be found at:
www.lion-publishing.co.uk